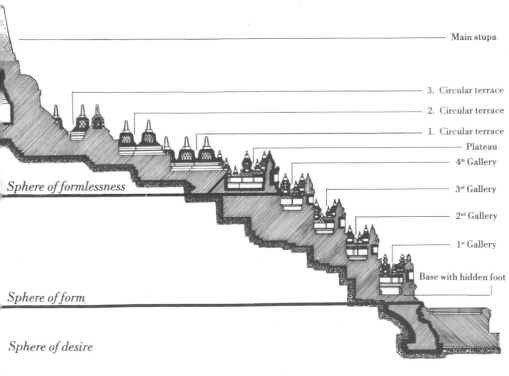

Main stupa

3. Circular terrace

2. Circular terrace

1. Circular terrace

Plateau

4ᵗʰ Gallery

Sphere of formlessness

3ʳᵈ Gallery

2ⁿᵈ Gallery

1ˢᵗ Gallery

Base with hidden foot

Sphere of form

Sphere of desire

FRIEZE

Also by Cecile Pineda

F A C E

CECILE PINEDA

VIKING

VIKING
Viking Penguin Inc., 40 West 23rd Street,
New York, New York 10010, U.S.A.
Penguin Books Ltd, Harmondsworth,
Middlesex, England
Penguin Books Australia Ltd, Ringwood,
Victoria, Australia
Penguin Books Canada Limited, 2801 John Street,
Markham, Ontario, Canada L3R 1B4
Penguin Books (N.Z.) Ltd, 182–190 Wairau Road,
Auckland 10, New Zealand

First published in 1986 by Viking Penguin Inc.
Published simultaneously in Canada

Grateful acknowledgment is made for permission to reprint
the following copyrighted material:

Two illustrations from *Borobudur* by Jurgen D. Wickert
published by PT Intermasa, Jakarta, Indonesia.

Excerpts from the *Reporter*, Vol. XIV, No. 5, May/June 1985
published by Barnard College.

LIBRARY OF CONGRESS CATALOGING IN PUBLICATION DATA
Pineda, Cecile.   Frieze.
I. Title.
PS3566.I5214F75   1986   813'.54   85-41083
ISBN 0-670-81179-3

Printed in the United States of America by
The Book Press, Brattleboro, Vermont
Set in Bodoni Book

In memory of my mother, Jane

The great pagoda is raised. The country lies ruined.

—BURMESE SAYING

For the fifth consecutive year, in the face of the highest child-poverty rate in eighteen years, our national leaders have targeted poor children and families again for billions in new budget cuts. . . . [Meanwhile] an escalating arms race and nuclear proliferation not only hold hostage the future we hold in trust for our children, but also steal the present from millions of the world's children whose principal daily enemy is relentless poverty and the hunger and disease it breeds.

—MARIAN WRIGHT EDELMAN,
quoted in
The Barnard Reporter

AUTHOR'S PREFACE

Borobudur first invaded my consciousness in 1984 when I spent a solitary hour scampering over the vast pyramid/stupa/shrine which lies on the Indonesian island of Java, in the near vicinity of Jogyakarta. What initially struck me was the vast scale of the monument, its ingenious conception, and the remarkable vitality of the stone relief work which, for depth of feeling and subtlety of execution, rivals anything known to the West.

Then, too, I was moved by what, even on first blush, seemed to be an argument between, on the one hand, the highly elegant iconography of those panels in all four galleries devoted to the lives of the Buddhas, and the astonishing vigor that animates depictions of the more vernacular Buddhist legends and animal fables.

My first impression was borne out by a visit to another, this time, Hindu, shrine in the same vicinity. Known as Prambanan, and completed some eighty years or so after Borobudur, it consists not of one, but of a cluster of shrine/pagodas, their exteriors decorated with stone reliefs, but whose subjects originate principally in the Hindu epic, the Ramayana. Again, I marveled at the extraordinary exuberance of the depictions, some of which show life much as it was lived over one thousand years ago, and is still lived among countryfolk throughout Asia, with patient honoring of time and season, with reverence for the animal and vegetal worlds paralleling the human and divine.

Frieze was first conceived as a rivalry between a master carver, traded to Java by an Indian dynast, and a native carver, recruited from a local village. But long before the first draft was completed four months later, quite another story was demanding to be told. I had discovered that Borobudur was raised with forced labor. The great number of Borobudur's builders were recruited from the rice fields.

Statistics pale against the actual vastness of Borobudur's scale. It required some one million carved stones, mostly of volcanic rock, to build, it measures one hundred thirteen meters corner to corner, and thirty-one meters high. For a temple of its size and period (the completion date hovers around 800 A.D.), Sanskrit sources relating to other monuments suggest that it may have required nearly ten thousand workmen to be on the site at any given time during the more than eighty years it took to build. For a feudal ninth-century agricultural society, the logistics of feeding and sheltering such a vast number, let alone organizing them into effective work gangs, rivals the complex organization and technology of a modern-day space launch.

Not long after Borobudur's completion, Central Java

collapsed economically and politically. It is known that the Sailendra dynasts, to whose glory Borobudur was built, were forced to abdicate, and that the new dynasty that replaced them, the Sanjaya, chose to set their capital far to the east, so depleted had become the heartland. Were the Sailendra bankrupted by their own extravagant monument building? The pattern of history seems to suggest such a course of events, but no one knows for sure.

The ancient world of ninth-century Asia saw a vigorous and extensive mercantile and tourist activity, although the latter was probably motivated more by religious fervor than sensation seeking. Economic organization, such as that found in India, where craftsmen were already grouped into guilds, could be highly sophisticated, contrasted, say, with Java, where the economic base was entirely agricultural. The custom of exchanging carvers, sculptors, painters, and decorators was frequently practiced by feudal monarchs who used such mutual favors to bolster their sometimes shaky political and economic alliances.

Apart from these generalities, there is little in *Frieze* that is not directly suggested by the monument itself: the hidden base, the pillaged great stupa, the one hundred twenty panels in the first gallery, meant to depict the life of Gautama Buddha from before his birth to the preaching of the First Sermon, and to provide the pilgrim who circled the gallery with a formal framework for his meditation. The growing of rice is never depicted on any of the panels that adorn Borobudur. Rice figures only on

richly laden tables, or as part of elaborate temple offerings. Forced abortion figures not only on one of Borobudur's hidden panels, but is to be seen at Prambanan as
well. For these monuments, like the great European
cathedrals, which they predate by nearly four hundred
years, are the books of vernacular history, depicting
myth and custom as they continue to be celebrated by
people who still live by the sweat of their brow.

The reader may perceive a nagging parallel between
that ancient world and his own, with one exception: it
will be the rare curiosity seeker who one thousand years
hence makes a tourist pilgrimage to a line of missile
silos, guidebook in hand.

The study of Borobudur is a fascinating one, and,
despite the recent UNESCO-sponsored restoration project, much about its construction remains a mystery,
unexplained by anything more substantial than conjec-
ture. For the reader who, like myself, cannot put the
subject out of mind, *Ageless Borobudur* by Augustus
Bernet-Kempers is recommended reading.

CECILE PINEDA

San Francisco
1985

CONTENTS

 SLANT THE CHISEL JUST SO, so that the hammer, tapping lightly on the shaft, lifts up the layers, flakes them off like skin. The workings are simple: everything depends on the angle, and the strike of the hammer blow; there are as many kinds as colors. Not so the stone. For in reality, no matter what the angle and type of instrument, or the skill of the hammer blow, the kind of stone, whether soft or hard, whether light or dark, decides. For all depends how daylight first strikes and moves with the passing hours over the surface of the face, and neither the finishing plaster, nor the colors applied by the painters afterward can redeem a bad design.

> Brahma, Siva, Vishnu
> are three;
> so chisel, hammer, and stone
> are three.

I had forgotten this song, forgotten we sang it over and over until the words lost all meaning, in the shed

3

of the master where we were given our first backgrounds to carve. Already the designs had been incised in the surface of the stone. To us fell the backgrounds, mine, the fig tree, heavy with fruit. Older apprentices would work the figures later.

Still now it is second nature: this ring of metal on stone, the clink, clink, the scatter of dust. Even now they tell me of the precision of the angle, how trued to the design.

There are limits. I have resigned myself to them: the great processions, the parallel forms of armies, hunters, suppliants, parasols, palm-leaf fans, royal standards, of fronds, of flowers, iridescent feathers, elephants propelled by the cruel hook thrusts of their mahouts; the palanquins, the gonfalons, the pavilions of pleasure, the dalliance of lovers under the awnings, the raising of the dead, the damned leaping in hellfire—all these I have renounced, abjured them as heresy.

Now there are only funerary ornaments, simple forms: finials, lanterns, pastimes fitting an old man. They suffer me, give my hands permission, gray my beard further with their dust. At least I am sheltered from the sun, from want. From where I sit by the roadside, I can smell the changing of weather, of season. When I pause to wipe my brow, I can hear the rumble of the oxcarts, or on still days, the beating of the threshers on the threshing floors, my harvest, the fragments of stone that scatter in my lap.

 "WHAT ARE YOU THINKING?"

I hear her sandals grate in the stone dust.

"Not thinking anything; hearing. Hearing, no more."

"Hearing? What do you hear?"

"Clink, clink." (I always hear it, even on cloudy days, even at night. Must hear it when I dream.) "Clink, clink."

"I heard you working in the night," she says. A reproach? Merely an observation?

"I couldn't sleep," I say.

She hands me the bowl. The grainy smell of rice assails my nostrils. Morning has made me hungry. "I brought you milk." I hear the bowl scrape the ground where she sets it down. I see it clearly, whether or not I fail to shut my eyes. For my lids still function: close, open. I have learned to keep them shut. I will stretch my arm just so. Unerringly my fingers will find the rim, my hand mold to the curve, raise it to my lips. I never spill a drop. Everything around me has its place. The shed,

5

the stone where I have left it to be dressed, the lanterns that line the roadway. I know exactly where, how many.

The stone stairs—three upward into the courtyard— the sleeping platform, the rolled mat, I sense them so keenly, I wonder have they come to roost in my head like hens clucking in the rafters. I trace my footfalls in the compound like dark lines etched upon a map. It is only when I leave the wall, negotiate the steps, crumbling now, at back, feel the unevenness of the ground slope downward, the grass blades cut my shins, searching out the ditch where I relieve myself—my certainties tremble on the verge of chaos.

A fart or two, I think, and all will come to rights.

FOR SOME TIME NOW I have been unable to sleep. In the early part of the night, my sleep is heavy, dull gray, as the smoky fur of moles or of night predators, devoid of dreams. I wake in darkness, start bolt upright. Perhaps I am on the edge of dreaming, unable to fall, to let myself fall into a world of color, of light that waits for me beyond this door. It is as if my eyes, even sleeping, cling to their blindness.

Dread? I ask myself of what. The days here stretch endlessly from season to season, marked only by the chill and wet of each monsoon. Of such blandness, perhaps. For I have always preferred the times of change, the first lightening of the eastern sky, the phosphorescent glow of twilight. And now, still now it is the sound of morning come at last, the first timid cries of birds welcoming my wakefulness, dispelling the darkness of the night, even now, it is this sound which stays with me best. It is as if I could almost see it, yet to picture it in my inner eye, I cannot. My sight is at a loss.

It was not always so. Carving my first design, the fig

7

tree, even then I could see the dentilation of the leaves, feel the fullness of the fruit, bristling with ripeness, the ghostly veining beneath the bloom. Finished, it was as if you could merely reach, and pluck. As if the stone itself promised sweetness to the tongue. Or the small lizard I cunningly concealed amidst the branches, sunning itself half hidden, at rest only for a moment before birdcry panicked its stone heart.

How had I done it? How was I to know? It came that way, perhaps because I saw it, smelled the summer air, breathed in the dust.

**4**

BRIMMING WITH FULLNESS I see it still: the clear water, its surface rocking against the rim, where Maya, my first wife, she of my heart, set it down, see it clearly still now, through the glass, a bowl of light. *Tell this in stone. See how you would trap it, make it shimmer with the play of sunlight.* How? Then I never asked, my chisel led me to it. Enchanted, perhaps? I let it. Why should I quarrel? It showed the way. I simply followed.

Or her hand, the particular taper of the fingers, or the curve of her neck as she bent over the water jar.

What is it I feel, here, in my chest? A splinter of cold? Why now? I never think of her. *Have you come back after so long, so far?* Why now? Why here? *Would I know you at all now—if you lived?*

"Gopal," she says, "come here. Come have a look."

She stands in the light of the doorway, turning slowly to show me. It is a new dress, the cloth filmy, threaded with gold. Her smile lights her eyes.

"Gopal, come look."

9

She stands in the sunlight of the doorway. Slowly she turns. The cloth, the threads of gold, her eyes: red, golden yellow, green. Slowly the cloth, the threads of gold, her eyes catch fire.

"Gopal, look!"

 "WHAT ARE YOU THINKING?" She stands beside my work mat, her sandals scraping the dust. I start in surprise. I had not heard her coming.

"Something I was remembering. A dress."

"Maya's?"

Her question catches me unprepared. We never talk of Maya—not since that first time. I nod.

"It must have been my master's house, still then. With the first money he gave me. She had bought a dress. Red. No. It was red or orange. Yes. Golden-yellow with threads of gold . . . green . . . I don't remember."

She says nothing. I wonder what she is thinking. I keep to my silence, waiting. She stands very quietly. Perhaps she is not thinking anything: even her sandals in the dust are still.

I want to whisper her name. But I find I cannot. Something holds me back. I reach my hand toward where she stands. But she gives no sign. There is no one there. She has gone quietly, making no sound. How is it possible? I think. In all this time, has she deliberately been scraping the dust to announce her presence, so as not to startle me?

 MY HANDS WEIGH HEAVY in my lap. The doorway is there again. Outside, in the courtyard, the sun beating against the powdery whiteness is blinding. But Maya is gone. The doorway is empty.

Curious. Why this apparition? Why now? after all these years. I feel a lassitude as if something had come to an end. Is it perhaps this dream that waited to visit me, and that, sleepless, I fled?

Dizzy with the heat, faint from the ride in the palanquin, the nausea rising with the smell of incense as I stumbled toward the welcome shade of the doorway to her father's house, I noticed neither the richness of the preparations nor the rice painting covering the floor in welcome. I remember only the dipper of cool water lifted to my parched lips in the shelter of the doorway. And she, veiled then, all but for the eyes, and in her shy glance, the betrayal of that secret smile: Maya. In my mother tongue her name signifies illusion. But to me, still now, it means fresh water.

 I CAME TO HER TREMBLING, was it with desire? More likely fear because she . . . . Mute, something in the eyes, a fluttering like the myna bird that time, nearly dead of fright when I plucked it from the cat's claws.

"What is it?"

"I am afraid."

"Of what?"

"Afraid you will send me back."

"Back? Why send you back when only just now . . . ?"

"Because I don't know what brides are supposed to do!"

I offered the tail of my nightshirt to her timid sniffle. In a burst of courage, she gave a mighty blow. A tide of giggles overtook her. We rolled in the waves of that terrifying bed, drowning in a sea of laughter. And then, at last . . . she looked to me for guidance. I was six years her senior. I was nineteen.

We lived in Gupta's house as is the custom, for he

was my master. Already then, with sixteen sons—all of them carvers or cutters of stone—he had room for one son more. We made our life in the small room which lay at the far end of the corridor, behind the kitchen. She brought her dresses with her in the cart and cooking vessels in a small carved chest. And as a special gift from her father's house—for she was his only daughter—a small chair painted in many colors and strung—as was our bed—with rope.

**8** Not a breath of air to stir the nets. Sated, we dozed in the master's pavilion with no one to wake us but the monkeys overhead. Monkeys! The air was raucous with their chatter. Sometimes, as I raised myself on my elbow to watch her sleep, her face became the rosy sandstone, my hands hummed with imagining the bite of the chisel gently chipping, molding the faint hollows at the corners of her smile, allowing the soft stone to flake like skin until it all but breathed with my first wife's dreaming, lying there, white, fragile in her nakedness.

The reliefs I copied slavishly still then, for I was young and still apprenticed, those smiles which until then I copied became my own: her celestial smile, the smile of centuries . . . and in the stone, I thought, it would last as long. People seeing it would remember for a thousand years.

Perhaps I imagined it, perhaps even now I am mistaken. But it seemed to me my carving took on new life, the forms took on a radiance of their own as if the stone itself held its breath before igniting, as if the stubborn dullness gave way to translucent eyes of light.

 MORE AND MORE she came to watch, her face veiled at first—all but the eyes, which saw everything. In no time she grew familiar: "Why not make the eyes like this, sly," and she would cast her eyes sideways above the veil, "as though they held a secret. People will never tire of looking then!" Or she would say: "Couldn't you give the figure a twist—here—like this—as if the dancer's body hadn't quite set, not quite yet, in the perfect pose? People will go mad to see her move! They will swear they hear the music play!" And her dark eyes would dance with relish at her stratagems.

My apprentices, who were her age, would laugh. They came to await her visits, eager to hear her laugh, to watch her pose. It was as if she read my mind, gave my ideas voice, for already then these things were known to me—like knowledge that comes with the bones, as Gupta, my master, used to say, with the marrow you are born with.

 THE CHANGE MUST have begun some time before I noticed it. She moved more slowly at first. She came to the site less and less. I remember my mother waving her finger—it must have been—after granny, the blind vegetable woman in the marketplace, had arranged the match.

"Gopal, Gopal, watch out. Even old granny makes mistakes. She is their only daughter. Her father let her do too much. As a child, he even taught her how to carve. Watch her carefully lest she grow restless."

The apprentices inquired after her at first. "Something has come over her," I would say by way of explanation. They would clap their sides at something that escaped me utterly. I would catch their smiles behind my back.

I had begun to notice her more carefully. I would see her paused in a doorway, or sometimes when she stood up, a look would come over her face, a sort of bemusement.

Later I came to know how my choice of words had betrayed my ignorance.

"It's moving, isn't it?"

"Yes. I feel him stirring," she would say. "It will be a boy, Gopal. I know it. It will be a boy."

 I SAT ON THE EDGE of the string bed where she lay on her side, propped on an elbow, her hand cradling the contours of her rounding form. The room was dark, sweltering.

"How is it, Gopal? Noon and already you are back?"

"I am puzzling something: the Lord Krishna is bathing in the stream. A river nymph pours water from a conch she holds tipped above his head. Small fry rollick at his feet. But the stream! The stream is what eludes me." I read to her from the *silpasastra*. " 'Water is of two kinds. Still water and agitated water, such as is seen before a storm. Still water signifies calm or peace. The lines must be wavy. Agitated water shows impending conflict. The lines must be jagged like waves in a choppy sea.' "

"Does it say nothing else?"

I shook my head. She lay quietly, musing. A look came over her, the same look I had lately come to know. Quite suddenly she leaped from the bed where she reclined now more and more. I could see her awkwardness as she fumbled with her slippers, but big as she was, she moved with surprising swiftness. I heard her move along the passage toward the kitchen. She was not gone long.

"Gopal," she called.

I followed the sound of her voice. On the window ledge she had set it down, the bowl of glass. She had filled it to brimming with our precious drinking water. She knocked it, brusquely, nearly tipping it.

"What are you doing!" I cried out in alarm.

I followed the movement of the water, now a pearl, now a mirror, now catching, now repelling the sunlight of the courtyard.

"There!" she whispered. "Tell this in stone!"

 A RESTLESSNESS VISITS me always at this time of year. The air is heavy with the smell of wet earth as if the deep itself had given up its moisture, and the sky, burdened with it, prepared to burst. And now I am without eyes, the smell is enough to remind my body. I tremble like an alley dog, succumb to shaking for no apparent reason.

And the dreams! All these visitors, these thoughts, colors where before there was gray . . . these too, may be the signals of impending rain. I consider: the stillness of the air, this waiting for the sky to burst. . . .

So it was then. On the string bed she lay gasping. The heat was more oppressive than ever I remember. The midwives stayed with her two days; the priest was summoned to make the offerings customary in such cases, and the sorceress, a wild woman of the country-side who made her drink a tea of forest herbs. No matter where I fled it seemed to me I could hear her moaning. For a long time after, her screams still echoed in my skull.

Our child was born as the first rains came. Squalls lashed the downpours, propelling them this way and that. The courtyard was quickly flooded. Wind gusts pocked the surface of the water.

It was a girl. When she saw it she turned her face to the wall and wept. "Take her away," she wailed to the midwife. "Take her away." And heedless of the tempest, sank into the deep and deathly slumber of exhaustion.

 Even when the rains ceased, she stayed in the darkened room. In broad daylight, she left the shutters closed. I would walk in on her sitting quite still on the low decorated stool she loved, her tiny hands folded listlessly in her lap. She stared straight before her. She sat like that for hours in the steamy darkness of the shuttered room. Gently I would try to lift her, carry her to bed, loose her clothing pin, unwrap the layer upon layer of filmy garments till she lay naked, passive, her dark eyes glazed, filmed over. I fed her with a golden spoon. Like a good child, she suffered it. Everything. Yet never was there sign she really noticed, acquiesced, or even recognized. It was as if her spirit fled, leaving the cocoon of her life hollow.

I caressed her, ran my hands fluttering over the spongy roundness of her young mother's belly, found the dark places of our joy. Patiently she suffered me. She gave no word, no cry. I made love to a broken doll, the strings loose, undone utterly. When I held her to me, only then she seemed to give a sign. Absently she would stroke my hair, cradle my head briefly before letting her arm drop listlessly at her side.

"Maya?"

I would enter the darkened room. She said nothing. Not I, not the steady drumming in the thatch could rouse her.

"Maya? Are you in pain?"

Sometimes she would whimper softly. She never really answered me.

I opened the shutters a crack. In the flooded fields, birds were returning, clinging precariously to the wisps of stubble. A steady drip fell from the rain-soaked thatch. I could see her, not moving, following the course of the raindrops with her eyes.

"WHAT HAS BECOME of the child?"
Gupta's question found me out in the
darkened passage of the corridor.
"They took her away."

"And you let them? Don't you know where she is?"

I, who had assumed she was exposed, who had never given her a passing thought, it was as if fear made my bowels drop between my knees. I began running. I didn't know where until I reached the vegetable stalls.

"Old Mother," I begged. "Tell me where she is. If you know it, tell me where they took her."

"Who?" Her blind eyes seemed to stare at me.

"The midwives. What have they done with my child?"

"Ah, it is you, Gopal."

It must have been the talk of the marketplace. Everyone knew but me. She had been taken by the midwives to be left to die. But it was said the wild woman, the one they called the sorceress, had found her in the forest and had taken her away. No one knew where.

 I TOOK DURGA TO WIFE, a village girl. Dark, this one, of a plainness quite unlike her of my heart. But a ready smile, firm, round flesh. A willingness to work, to run my household when we left my master's house.

I was away at first light. The daylight must be used from first to last, for without it, all work ceased. I carved steadily. At midday, I stopped only long enough to eat the rice she brought me every day, cooked and spiced to perfection. At dusk, when I returned exhausted, she always waited to greet me in the courtyard. She took the bundle of empty dishes from my hands. She poured cool water from the clay jug on my head and neck. She lifted a clean garment over my head.

Who knows? To say I loved her? Now in my age, I wonder. Then I was sure I knew. For where were the cries in the night? In her good-natured bustle, her patience, where was the trembling? I never watched her sleep. Perhaps it was she who watched my dreaming. Perhaps she lay awake beside me, patiently waiting till I should rouse myself, unwilling or afraid to rise before me. Perhaps it was she watching; my hollowness visited me only with phantoms.

Two sons she bore me. She watched over them, over the household, and over my loved one. Sometimes I would follow her movements in the next room, bathing her, dressing her, bringing her sweetmeats, or a special, particularly sweet morsel, oiling her hair, talking to her, my loved one, in soft tones, flattering, cajoling, making pleasantries, until at last one day, I heard a hollow sound. At first I took it to be weeping or hiccuping that seemed to come from very far. But it was my loved one laughing.

I sat in the neighboring darkness. When at last she found me there, my head sunk in my hands, all she would say is, "Don't. Don't. She's happy. Didn't you hear her laughing? Don't you know she's happy?"

MORE AND MORE I stayed away, unable to see the ghost that stayed behind as if to taunt me, to torment my memory of summer, of the pavilion, of our joy under the nets. I wonder now if I had stayed would it have made a difference.

I buried myself in the stone, forgot about the child. But even the building site could not provide escape forever. Carving became a drudgery. The lightness seemed to vanish, the figures lay stiff, wooden in the stone, their smiles frozen, grotesque. The apprentices no longer asked for news of her. They came to avoid my troubled eyes. We went about our work with a kind of doggedness, without thought, like winches that raise water from a village well, every day the same.

Dreams visited me—curious, unexplained. Sometimes they brought respite. Dreams of color, dancers clad in indescribable garments over bodies that were twisted or ill-formed. Or once I dreamed of a flower, unknown to me, its coppery leaves glistening with wet. Rain must have fallen in the night, yet I had felt nothing.

Surely the earth was soaked, but when I reached under
the fan of spreading leaves, the tuft came loose in my
hand, without any roots to hold it. I could not recall its
name—this spike of perfectly blue flowers. Regret visited me with a pang worse than any hunger.

 IN SUCH TIMES AS I have imagined I could not be more downcast, something almost always transpires to make me wish each former grievance could be recaptured a hundredfold. What seems beyond pain itself turns out to be some kind of ease. So it was then. Already when we left the master's house, there were rumors. It was said the neighboring kingdom was at war on our border. It was not quite five day's journey—too distant to concern us. Or so we thought. Life went on, the seasons came and went.

My sons were not yet five years old when the first horsemen came charging through the trees bordering the river. They seemed to rise up from the mist, ghost warriors. Surprised in the forest, women screamed. They need not have worried: rape and plunder would come later, when the expedition had slaughtered the sentries at the gate and left the city ruined. Only the temple was left standing, perhaps because they professed the same worship as we, perhaps because unlike the habitations of men, it was built of stone.

All work ceased, for there was no one to guarantee our *kalam* of rice. We waited. I could not fault Durga when it came to foresight: she had enough stored in our jars to last a month.

 Rumors came of a new expedition, this one from the south. My Lord of Chola rode with his army, extracting tribute as he came. All along the route, his vassals, at war with one another, knelt at his feet, suing for loans. Vaguely, my Lord of Chola promised them supplies. As guarantee, he helped himself to land.

I remember our outrage when he finally appeared in our midst, for he urged his horse over the rock pile and into the sacred courtyard itself, pointing here and there, trading shouted comments with his equerry. Before my carving of the Lord Krishna bathing, he reined in.

"Who did this?" he called. There was no answer. We stood cowering behind the rock pile.

Then he shouted, "What luckless mother's son?"

Gupta approached to where the horses stood tossing their manes.

"Sire, that is the work of our youngest master, Gopal, who stands there where you see him."

With a toss of the head, my Lord of Chola beckoned me closer. "You return with us. You join our caravan tonight. Hanh!"

He punctuated almost every phrase with this expletive as I was to learn. Nor was it a cough or hiccup. I had never heard anything the like. Then I did not wonder at it: there was rice left in our jars for three days more.

"And my household?" I wonder now where I found the voice. I was little over twenty then.

He leaned toward me as he wheeled his horse. A wheezing sound came from him. I took it for laughter. "Isn't my favor enough for you, hanh? Very well, then: they may accompany us. You have till nightfall to make ready."

 AT FIRST I wondered: what sky was this under which I slept? The stars were of the cold brilliance of gems, sharper than ever I remember them. The air was chill. I could see tents dotting the barren fields, like mushrooms sprung up in the night. The animals, freed of the traces, stood sleeping, dreaming of the grass. I searched for the others I knew must be sleeping there. But the mat I sought was empty. Maya was gone.

I started up anxious. My eyes searched the darkness. Beyond the wagons someone was running, disturbing the stubble in the ditches. The wick of an oil lamp fluttered and went out.

"Maya," I whispered. My voice was hoarse.

Out of the darkness I can still see her face swimming up toward me, ghostly in the night. She fell sobbing at my feet.

"What happened? Tell me."

"Gopal, Gopal. They are all there sleeping, mountains of young men."

"Did someone hurt you?"

"They are dead. All of them dead."

 PERHAPS IT BEGAN THERE, this journey into night, perhaps it was then: the point where return was no longer possible, return, if return could be, to something remembered or something perhaps that never really was.

Looking back, it seems to me that everything had color at the beginning: the sweetness of the days following one another, the sandstone, the stoneyard, the candy vendor beating his water harp—bright color, as if childhood ran way past its time, playing tag with rainbow powder, every day a feast.

Yet when I think, before the darkness—my own— long before. . . . Some gray dawn—not just the stone— overtook me in mist, exiled me to a world of black or gray, condemned me to pry apart the porousness of a stone gone dark, forgetful of the fire that gave it life, that spilled it from the stony womb of earth and sent it coiling down dark hillsides, trailing sparks in the night with each sweep of its serpent robes, stone tongues licking, devouring the rice, setting fire to whole villages, entombing the living with the dead, feeding, ravening, till sated, it curled up at last and went to sleep.

Even now, touching it, prodding it with my chisel, even disguised in the commonplace of these ornaments for hire, does the stone remember? Does the chisel remind it of the fire?

 On its floors of darkness, I watched the night thresh fireflies. The air was alive with them.

"What is she looking for there in the darkness? Do you know?"

Durga's question put me off. "Why? Why ask me?"

"There is something. She is looking for it, I am sure."

"The child, perhaps. It was a girl."

Durga said nothing. I heard only her breathing.

EVEN BEFORE our household was installed in the far pavilion bordering the palace wall, Maya went searching in the night. Each of us saw her. At first I believed she was awake. But Durga said she slept and must not be awakened lest she die.

"Of what?" I asked.

"Of grief that it is this world she inhabits, not another."

We sat quietly nodding before sleep.

"She is calling to it."

"Calling?"

"Her child. Yes."

We could hear her stirring. Instantly Durga started up awake. "She has given her a name," she whispered as she rose soundlessly from the mat. "The name of one perfectly blue flower."

 WITH AS MUCH CLARITY as if I had only just now stepped over the wooden threshold, I see the opening. It is low so that even one of my stature must bend forward a little to avoid the certain impact of the lintel overhead. For the openings here are framed of hardwood, expertly joined.

The doorway is not so much boarded up as obliterated by long disuse. The door itself as it squeals open on its decaying pins shows signs of infestation, of boring from within.

A major domo conducts masons and plasterers through the endless passageways, but I, the carver, see my opportunity. The crumbling wood yields to the pressure of my palm. In a moment I am over the threshold. Quietly I pull the door shut behind me. What will they imagine, entering from distant rooms to see me standing perfectly still in a chamber sealed to all appearances these many years?

The room within is dark. Its narrow window slit admits only enough light to reveal its boundaries: tiny, narrow, cellular. I have time before they come upon me. My eye scans the point where wall and ceiling join. I expect to discern traces of a frieze running the periphery of the room, a painting or design of red lacquer detailed in green and black and gold. My eye probes the darkness. But there is nothing there. Only mildew—or is it soot?

 I LIE LISTENING to the dawn wind in the bamboo. The dream still holds me in its dark embrace and will not let me go. From where had it come to me that after I left for Kedu, the Chola palace burned, that everything was consumed by fire? What I have forgotten, the dream now brings to mind. Why now? It leaves me curiously troubled. By what? I remember my joy at learning of the Chola's ultimate eclipse—he who traveled by night so none of us might see the ruin of our countryside, the fields laid waste, our best young men lying dead among the grasses that still now must sway taller, greener than the rest.

Can it be the nearly thirteen seasons I spent immured in the small cubicles of the women's quarters, like hen coops in a chicken yard? The rising before first light, crossing the sleeping palace courtyards, the towers ghostly, still clothed in mist? And the endless corridors, the endless friezes, demigods locked in furious embrace, their stone sighs filling the walls, the corridors. And the stone—not the rosy sandstone of my mother country this

—but black, spewed from its crucible of fire. The windows giving on a courtyard whose light blinded the eye, yet the slits so narrow I carved by torchlight, not just at dawn, but at high noon and all the day until shortly before dusk when I put the chisel down at last.

The sutras: my torment, for with each completed chamber—and they were clustered dense as honeycomb —came gifts of clothes and brass and sweetmeats. But what others imagined to be my good fortune proved as much my agony; for all gentleness, all guilelessness in those designs bore the enigmatic smile of Maya, she who sat, year after year, hands locked, frozen in her lap, who went on searching in the night.

 Durga always saved her the best morsels. . . . What drove her? Was it hunger perhaps?

Every night we heard her rummaging in the corners. Although the nights were filled with stars, Durga never saw them. She went following her—in the passageways, out into the courtyard. She dogged her every footstep lest she wake. For waking she might die.

My resentment grew and rankled. Perhaps she heard the blackness gathering in my heart. *Send her away.* Was it not the natural thing? Brides who were barren, ill, or otherwise useless: send them back to their father's house. There was some disgrace, but what of that? She would survive it. She might become herself again.

But Durga. It was as if she could read my thoughts. She said nothing. But quietly, she distanced herself. It was nothing I could make out clearly. It was more in a tone of voice, a look. She would spend long hours combing Maya's hair, soothing her with the warm water she heated patiently over the kitchen fire. I was left alone to catch sight of them from time to time through the open door.

**26** THE SEASONS CAME, following one another. Somewhere Maya found a homespun sack. She carried it with her, searching in the night. Like the leaf borer, my chisel gnawed its way along the passageways of the women's quarters, completing one chamber after another. At last I came to the grandest of them, the key to all the rest. It lay at the heart of the harem, destined to become the favorite's.

I remember with what relish I planned the cycle—forty-eight depictions were to adorn the walls, twelve poses to a wall, each related to the one preceding, so that reading from right to left, as is our custom, the lovers appeared to flow without weight or effort from one transition to the next and back to the beginning. Each posture was to represent a passing half-hour of pleasure in a day-become-eternal through the transforming power of love.

Nor was that all. I envisioned a further refinement, for the north wall was to be reserved primarily for vertical poses, the south for horizontal, with the east and west walls providing a kind of equinox in which roles reversed from supine to prone while bridging the transition from standing to reclining.

I remember still the perverse relish with which I anticipated the result. Would I still find it as intriguing now? Surely it was a series which when complete might have satisfied a gymnast. But pondering it after this fading lapse of time, leaves me hollow, a taste more bitter in the mouth than this dawn alone could bring.

 My LAST chamber was not quite yet complete at the time of the dedication. For the ceremonies had been scheduled early—before the rains—so as not to dampen the fire displays.

The Chola had declared the day a holiday. We had been present from the earliest dawn. My sons took their places with the young apprentices. Maya stood to one side where I could neither see nor hear her.

The sun in the lists was unsparing. But during the ceremonies we were to stand without a murmur. The royal horsemen must stage their games while we groundlings, deprived of the shade provided by the brightly colored awnings of the stands, must somehow withstand the heat, the long hours of waiting. True, the water carriers passed from time to time with their golden ladles. I still remember the bent heads, the parched mouths greedily sucking at the dippers.

Toward noon, when the sun was long past enduring, Maya pressed through the barriers before Durga could run after her to stop her. She staggered onto the sand of the playing field, momentarily empty of horsemen. Then, with all the court watching, she fell to her knees in the dust.

"Who is this woman?" The Chola's angry shout voiced a question I had long been pondering to myself. "Take her away!"

When the royal guard had her surrounded, it was Durga who stopped them from laying hands on her. In the sudden hush, her shout echoed through the empty playing field: "No!"

I moved forward then, staggered more likely. The guards parted ranks to let me pass.

"She is my wife. She is Maya, my wife."

The Chola appraised me with a cold eye. "One *kalam* less for the carver's household. Hanh!" And with a clap of the hands he turned his attention to the games.

**28** WITH ONE *KALAM* less, there was not enough for the five of us. Who knows? If Gupta had not come south with all of his sixteen sons, I might even then have sent her back. But with the palace nearing completion, the Chola dreamed up another project. It was to be a temple unlike any seen before. Its scope required a superintendent, architects, masons, and stonecutters. Gupta was summoned from the north.

"Gupta!" I ran forward to meet him. We embraced. We discovered we were crying. For through my long apprenticeship we had been as father and son. He was now nearing fifty, but he moved with surprising grace, as one of half his years.

"And life in the north, how is it under the Chola?" And so I heard it: hardship, hunger, whole families dying, carvers we had known, Maya's people among them. There was nowhere to send her anymore.

 Soon there was nothing left in our jars to make up the difference. Then it was Gupta who took to visiting us by night, bringing sweet cakes from his household.

"Taste, taste," he would urge.

But for all his cheerful encouragement, I could not bring myself to eat.

"What shall I do? What would you do?"

"Plead with him," he urged. "Everyone here knows: she is sick. Plead with the Chola."

"But will he listen?"

"Why should he not? The women's quarters place him forever in your debt!"

"It may be this very debt that causes difficulty. In all the carvings, he may recognize her face!"

"Her face?"

"How can I put it?"

"Speak plainly: say it!"

"I cannot help what I do. In every face, in each expression, there is something of her. It comes without my knowing or wanting it."

5 1

His air turned solemn. "I know, my son," I could see his face by lamplight, the sudden sadness even in that light.

"I know how that can be."

 "GOPAL, THE JARS are empty!" In the courtyard Durga waited for me with the water jug. "Shouldn't you plead for us?"

"Plead, plead. Everyone says plead," I shouted, furious, the water running in my eyes. "All right. Tell me. How? How, I ask you? And will the Chola listen? Can you tell me?"

"She is *sick*!" I had never seen her like this. "Surely anyone can see it. She lives dreaming of another place!"

"You go." I said it more in jest than seriously. "You tell him, you who are only a country woman. Maybe you can move him. Maybe he will listen—and your face will cause him no offense!"

 THERE WAS SOMETHING in her look. Defiant? Perhaps not. But something. She stood before me, stood, yes, as if she were already somewhere separate from where I sat cooling myself.

"He says you are to come yourself!"

"What took you, woman?" I saw her features harden in the shadow of the coming twilight.

"It was you who said I should!"

"Yes. Jesting, only jesting."

"Ah, Gopal. Isn't it enough? How can we go on like this? As long as there was some rice left, we could just manage. And now . . . I put my head in the lion's mouth . . . and you . . ."

"And you . . . what?"

"*You did nothing!* Why are you never satisfied? What would it require? And if you were, would you let things rest?"

"Come inside," I said, rising. She followed me away from the public courtyard.

"You are tired," I said.

"No, no. It is not that. I am tired, yes. But it is not that." She had traded her peasant calm for something I had never seen before.

Slowly she unfastened her veil and let it fall into her lap. "He has something to say to you. And you alone."

 "WHERE IS THE carver fellow, hanh?"
The room overflowed with courtiers all straining to have a look.
"Clear the way."

Servants, courtiers, all elbowed one another pressing through the tiny doors. In the room I stood at last, alone before the Chola.

"Do you know why I sent for you?" I thought of Durga. "What is the meaning of this?" He fastened his gaze on the friezes circling the favorite's chamber. "Can you explain it? I have women here from every one of my subject provinces. And this . . . this image is the only one you could find it in yourself to limn?"

"Sire?"

"A poor idiot, a crazy woman, hanh! You must share her affliction!"

"She is my wife. It is nothing I can help."

"Already with one *kalam* less . . . perhaps it should be two!"

"Even now we go hungry."

"If there is not enough to eat, why not send her

home. Even healthy women grow tiresome sooner or later."

"There is nowhere left to send her. All her people are gone." I said as little as possible. He did not need reminding of the famine. He began to wheeze with what I took at first to be fury. I might have known better: it was his way of laughing.

"Very well then," he choked. "Since the faces move you to excess, let us see you labor the backsides!"

He insisted that each female representation display the mark of his favorite, for she was said to bear a captivating mole (no one publicly professed to know where). His delight at my new torment knew no bounds. Each day, he came accompanied by courtiers. He offered suggestions, examined each new seal of royal approval.

"A little more round . . . like this," he would say. "It should make the mouth water. Hanh!"

 No SOONER had the last mole been rounded off to his satisfaction, than the Chola lost no time moving our household outside the palace compound. We took up quarters with others of the carvers' brotherhood near the river temple site. Gupta arranged with the project paymaster that I would join my name to my sons' on the temple roster.

"All the same, no faces for you! There is sufficient trouble here already," joked Gupta. "Shape the Apsarases for the niches overhead, but leave the carving of faces to another—my son Ganesh, perhaps. His talent is sufficiently modest not to give offense!"

At first, he had me working in the shed where there was shade. There were over one hundred Apsarases to be carved, every one the same. My days became sluggish with resentment. I turned edgy. Some days I struck the stone so roughly it broke open like burnt fruit. I would cast the pieces on the rock pile and try anew. Other times, preoccupied, I struck too softly. The stone stayed sullen, mute. My thoughts turned dark, porous as the stone.

 "IT IS TIME you served as under superintendent." Gupta's announcement was long in coming, but all the more welcome. "You will take charge of the apprentices."

It was the mark of his esteem, of our long-lasting friendship. And something else, perhaps. Already he had been at work on the river temple some eight years. He was turning gray about the temples. And although he walked briskly still, he had begun to stoop.

We sat together in the shade under the shed's overhang. He unfolded a scroll before us on the sand. Basement and cornice friezes were carefully drawn out, each panel sharply reduced in scale.

"You will take charge of these," he pointed to the sections already nearing completion. "Assign the apprentices as seems best to you." He glanced up at me as he helped me gather up the scroll. "Take it. It is yours."

 IN MY EAGERNESS to tell Durga, I remember taking the shorter way home, heedless of the rougher ground beneath my feet. The path followed the edge of the river, ran past the market stalls and gaily decorated river boats, for that particular day was market day. Small skiffs rode at anchor by the riverbank while the owners hawked their wares. All around me, the color, the shouts of the hawkers, the soft air, oblivious to them all, my thoughts were fastened on the midday meal, on the steaming rice I knew awaited me. Why I noticed the stall with its display of dresses fluttering like bright sails in the sunlight—why I noticed it at all, I am not sure. Probably the color attracted me. It may bring a smile to Maya, I thought. I selected the most exquisite. It was of the translucence of dragonfly wings, of the color of certain bubbles about to burst.

Only at the doorstep when I caught sight of Durga crouched, fanning the cooking fires, I remembered I had brought nothing for her. She rose when she caught sight of me in the doorway.

"Here," I said, offering her the dress. "I have brought you this."

"For me?" She let the dress unfold. She looked at me uncertainly. "Did something happen?"

"Gupta has made me carving superintendent."

Her smile of pleasure broke loose.

"I am to take charge of the apprentices."

 I HAVE HEARD it said of me that I drove them without mercy. But what choice had I? Caught between the limits of his workers' strength and the readiness of the newly set facings, a good superintendent must do whatever is required to uphold the schedule. The season came when, as we labored to complete the eastern side, the façade giving on the roadway, we first heard the rumors: the Chola had set aside a day when he—and all the court accompanying him—would come to view the work in progress.

Preparations of necessity were hasty. Gupta desired no time be spared. But others, led by Dudam, the building superintendent, won over him. It was decided to erect brightly colored awnings to shield the notables from the sun. Flowers would be gathered for scattering along the pathways in the temple courtyard.

But when the day arrived, I had contracted a fever and lay shivering in my bed. I vaguely remember my sons returning home long before sundown. In my delirium I feared they had been summoned home to watch

me die. As she sponged me with the cooling water,
Durga soothed my anxiety. "The river temple brings the
Chola great joy. He has made today a holiday!"

 I COULD NOT not remember where I lay. My eyes opened on a room already filled with light. My body seemed to float, but my eyelids were heavier than stone. A woman, more beautiful than any I remembered, bent over me, calling my name.

"Gopal."

Then it came to me. The fever had broken. And what I took at first to be a vision was Maya, but Maya more beautiful than I remembered even from the first days of my knowing her. I lifted my head from the pillow. The bed strings groaned in protest. I could see she wore the dress of gossamer wings. I was much surprised. I remembered clearly giving it to Durga. Yet here was Maya in colors more iridescent than glass, offering me water from the dipper—cooler, fresher than any I remembered.

 FOR SOME TIME after I took my place again on the site, I wondered. I could see Durga sometimes avoid my eyes, as if she hid something. One evening we sat in the shadow of the doorway. I am not sure what impulse took me. "Did you give it to her?"

"What?"

"The dress? The dress I brought for you. Did you give it to her?"

"To Maya? Why?"

"She was wearing it."

"She wore it? When?"

"When I awoke. I awoke from the fever. Maya was calling me. She gave me water from the dipper."

In the half-light I saw something come over Durga as she listened. Her expression seemed to cloud over, her eyes became opaque.

"It was I who called you. It was I myself."

TWO MORE SEASONS came and went. The friezes neared completion but for the borders, undemanding scrollwork—a job for the apprentices. Overhead the niches still gaped empty. Erecting the hoist was a matter of a few days more at most. Even now the head builder was seeing to assembling the parts. There was the peculiar restlessness and unease we always feel when any work comes to an end, a kind of nervous flurry of activity. And the building site swarmed with rumors. It was said His Lord of Chola planned another project somewhere in the south, which until now had been kept vague —a new palace perhaps, in an altogether different place. A summer pavilion by the eastern sea, or perhaps—and this came to me from the chief builder himself who may have had cause to know something unknown to any other—a new imperial city, a project of such vastness work gangs and stonemasons would have to be recruited from each one of the Chola's subject provinces—as I was once in the days following my apprenticeship. When I was summoned, rumors spread like fire. Everyone knew something was afoot.

"Perhaps he will offer you some new commission, name you chief builder."

"We will see," I said to Gupta. I was thinking: if I become the Chola's chief *silpin,* once more I plan my own designs. But answering to the royal whim I become every bit his slave. Better for myself—and for my sons —to remain free of the treasury's caprice. Let him find one who is more willing, with less knowledge than myself.

Gupta must have read my thoughts. "Why fret?" he counseled. "See first what it is that he intends. It may be like nothing you imagine. Your concern now will yield no benefit."

"When will you return?" Dudam, the chief builder, sat pondering the schedule.

"I am not sure. It depends how long I have of waiting. It depends on what I learn. It may be tonight, tomorrow." I shrugged. A shiver overtook me, a wave of cold, as of a cloud suddenly passing.

"You will see. It may be you will learn something of what it is he plans."

 THE DAY WAS SUNNY, the air light despite the heat. In the shimmer of leaves following the river's course, small birds chattered before the rumble of our wheels set them in skittering flight. Even the dragonflies hovered, darting this way and that in close unconcern.

It will work out. You will see.

Gupta's words emptied my mind of all but the tread of the bullocks, the susurrus of wheel on dust, of birdsong in the branches, of the wind's caress, of the sunlight, of the gold. . . .

 THE GATEKEEPER reached a hand to help me from the wagon, more by way of formality. It was not so high I could not find my own way to the ground. In the inner courtyard, a basin was laid out. A court woman dipped a conch in cool water to wet my face, my hands, in a ceremony born of riding dusty roads. I smelled the fragrance over my hair, my scalp. But my thoughts were on the inner room, on the dark within, which, try as they might, my eyes failed to penetrate.

I remember the cool under my feet and the hardness of the marble that sent barbs shooting as I knelt. How long am I meant to prostrate myself thus? I wondered. But the faint prod on my shoulder called me to be seated. I found I had forgotten, now it was upon me, what it was I was meant to say.

Two attendants moved from the shadows bearing between them a great vessel filled to overflowing. For a moment only, I guessed at some mockery. But the Chola spoke: "You have served us well: the river temple, our *women's quarters* (he stressed the word 'harem' as if it

encoded some mischief we held secret between us). Still
now the *sutras* (again the stress) bring us many hours of
happy amusement. Hanh!" He allowed a slow smile to
play about his lips. "You have served us well these
twenty years. . . ."

Twenty! How easily we accept the yoke! Twenty
monsoons. Curious how we become so sunk in the pursuit of craft, so harmless, while *they*!—playing with
kingdoms, whole peoples, with never a thought. Issuing
orders, keeping records, counting out measures of grain,
of sheep, with the same efficiency they use to pluck a life
—or a way of living—thinking of nothing but making
profit whether by war, or husbandry, it matters little
which.

". . . to trade builders. So it is our pleasure to trade
you for another." I heard him come to a stop. I realized
with alarm I had heard nothing of what he said.

"It is time we showed our allies, these Sailendra,
they are not the sole builders in the East. Let them see
what riches we have guarded so jealously in our midst.
From your own experience you know the worth of a good
carver."

It was an alliance he planned, he the master of
shifting alliances, with me as bait. His silence gave me
permission. "These kings . . ."

"The Sailendra . . ." he prompted.

"These Sailendra . . . Where? . . . in what region do
they hold sway?

"In Kedu. But already their influence is felt not only
in their home island of Chopo, but throughout the ar-
chipelago, the mainlands—even here."

I knew nothing of Kedu. I knew only vaguely it was an island kingdom in the eastern sea.

"Your willingness to be visited by their emissary gives us much pleasure. . . ."

I had said nothing of willingness. And what concern was that to him, he who thought of nothing but making war—or peace—when it served him, trading artisans, disrupting whole households merely to decorate a harem wall.

"What plans has he for my household?"

The bluntness of my question appeared to stun him.

"Household? There is no provision for traveling with a household. Ever. Such arrangements are far too inconveniencing."

"Then I beg you will excuse me. I desire nothing so much as following the brotherhood to another site."

The Chola never shifted his expression. "Very well."

**As it had been,** I thought, our life would go on without disruption. From what I understood of such things, in matters where artisans were traded, it was always the custom of the reigning dynast to pay whatever expense was necessary. But for traveling, it was the Chola who must pay, and clearly I had won my reprieve only because he was unwilling. And so the matter would rest.

As I entered the doorway, my eyes pulsed with the blinding light of noonday. The room sweltered in darkness. The shades were lowered and made fast against the heat. Durga was not there. My eagerness to tell her, tell anyone, gave way. A kind of disillusion came over me quite suddenly. I felt alone. No matter, I thought. It will pass. I slumped down on the decorated seat Maya loved so well.

"What did he say?" she wanted to know.

"My King of Chola? Nothing. Just that he planned to trade me for another."

I had imagined the scene, had rehearsed it all the

long way home, as I sweltered under the overhang. But there was no one there to hear it.

Abruptly I rose, tumbling the stool aside. I set it to rights. I would make my way to the site. Gupta was waiting. I would tell him—and Dudam—what it was I knew.

I picked my way over the rock pile. The carvers were busy with the final touches, the hoist had been assembled already since morning. Despite myself, I felt excitement. I am finished here, I thought, now the temple building is coming to an end. But the Chola will busy us all with his new project, a palace, or a new city, perhaps. There will be ample opportunity.

"Gupta!" I shouted above the din. I saw him come scampering toward me over the rock pile, moving with lightning energy for someone of his sixty years.

"He desired to trade me," I shouted.

He came abreast of me. He was smiling. "And you accepted!"

"No. I refused." His face took on an air of puzzlement.

"You refused? Then why has your name been stricken from the paymaster's roster?"

"Stricken? When?"

"This morning. Dudam has expressly been so informed. The Chola's message came today."

 "THERE IS NO MISTAKING THEM." I can see the emissary straddling the bench as if he still rode the curiously caparisoned mare which even now stood tethered, pawing the ground beside the post. In the shed, rows of stone Apsarases stood, their necks thin and curved like the flower stalks they offered to the sweltering air, waiting for the hoist. I noticed one of them still stood faceless.

"The panels, the friezes, I know your hand."

In the sudden obscurity of the overhang, there was something about this Shanggal that eluded me at first. Only slowly did my eyes make out the net of fiber that obscured his face. I began to discern his features more clearly through the veil. His nose had the peculiar flatness occasioned by the restraint of the cloth he wore tied behind his head.

"My Kings, the Sailendra, look to you not for decoration (he said this pejoratively), not for decoration, as you are wont to think of it here, working for these little Chola kings, mere Pallava vassals. They look to you for the very heart of the mystery: one hundred and twenty friezes carved in stone, friezes to depict the life of the Enlightened One. The first gallery will be yours entirely, the most important. Nor will you lack for assistants. You will have full rein: one hundred, two hundred, perhaps a thousand—on a project of such magnitude. But if you think of temples, erase such thoughts. This will be like nothing known to you: a world, a cosmic mountain, a model of the universe!"

I watched him struggle to pull a scroll from his saddlebag. "The Lalitavistara of Siddhartha Gautama!" he announced. I strained to make out the unfamiliar script in the obscurity. "And that other?" I pointed to the scroll lying deep in the saddlebag.

"That is the Jatakamala." And seeing that I did not understand, "The legends. The lives of he who is to become Buddha. . . . But we have our local people at work on those already. They need be of no concern to you. Your panels will show the life of the Holy One from before his birth to the first earthly manifestation: the First Sermon beside the holy river. Just that." He waved a jeweled finger vaguely to indicate the scroll I held in my hand.

Even through the veil, he had a way of looking, this Shanggal, that held the eyes.

"Are you equal to it?"

I returned his look. "Certainly the equal. More than the equal."

I can see his smile still. "So much the better. My Kings, the Sailendra, offer three measures of rice for you

—and for your assistants. And ten pieces of gold at the successful completion."

Ten! I was careful not to show my surprise. The offer of gold was not customary with us.

"And for my household . . . ?" I looked at him without flinching.

"You intend to take your household?"

I nodded.

"My orders say nothing of that. But I can arrange it. Of that I have no doubt!"

 Now I WONDER if I would see things differently. Would I be more wary? Or would I as easily succumb to the honor done me? to the flattery? For how could he have recognized my hand, this Shanggal, emissary to the Sailendra, when he concerned himself then—as he may still now—with the buying and selling of whatever comes to hand: people, influence, whole provinces— anything that could be bought or sold or traded. What would you call such a one? Not a man, surely. A merchant-assassin? Is the term too harsh?

I remember thinking that men of his country must wear the veil when they traveled to protect them from the dust. Only when we were aboard ship bound for Kedu I began to wonder. I remember thinking it was strange that he should wear it where the air was pure.

And much later, later than I knew I would, when I came to know something more of this Shanggal, I began to wonder—as I do now. So much, so much is never known to us, not with any certainty, is not given to us to know. Had he offered me ten gold pieces perhaps because he himself had been assured of twenty? And why, why is it that I should end my days here, without eyes? But wait! Perhaps already you have guessed it, as long before I entered the courtyard at sunset, I trembled at what I would find.

What is she looking for there in the darkness? What? The child? Perhaps. It was a girl. She has given it a name. Or that time: *They are dead, Gopal, all the young men. Dead.* No, no. That is not it. Not it at all. Durga. It was Durga at the heart of it: *You did nothing! I put my head in the lion's mouth. And you did nothing. You are never satisfied. And if it were given, would you rest? Would you let it rest? And now . . . ?*

Everything, everything imagined twists itself in the dream of fate. Fate itself is dreaming, only dreaming, and you, all, all dreaming.

How was it i knew? Already as I stepped over the raised threshold of the courtyard, something was amiss. I looked for Durga where she always waited, her watering jar ready. It did not surprise me that no one was there.

I entered the darkened room (*what snared bird is this that still now knocks against my ribs?*). The decorated seat was empty. I noticed the paint had chipped away. No one sat there, no pale drawn face, no hands pressed tight in the lap, or perhaps working at a wisp of straw.

It may be better this way, I thought.

Maya! Someone was sobbing in the courtyard. I could hear it distinctly. I had not made a sound. From where I sat slumped I could see the courtyard in the sun's last rays. The whitewashed walls were golden with evening. Blue shadows reached almost to where I sat.

Already the far side lay in darkness. Who was it I saw there now, leaning against the well? Was that my son? Was that Govind I saw there? As I came abreast of him, I caught sight of his reflection far down in the

7 9

pool of still black water. Only his hair was burnished, fired by the setting rays of sunlight.

"Govind," I whispered, "tell me."

"Tell you what?"

"Tell me what you know."

"Nothing." He eyed me dully. He wiped his nose on his sleeve.

Were these my fingers tearing savagely at the golden hair?

"They have gone! They left for Durga's village! In the north! It is a sorceress they seek!"

"Govind." I let go his hair. "It must be a year already you have been sniveling at this well. See how even now the water level rises."

But my sob caught me out. What foolishness. What foolishness. Why is it we grasp at straws? When the moment prods us with its pain, we think nothing of jesting, of masking the face of the heart.

I had not known I would even weep.

 FROM FAR BACK in the compound, I can hear my wife's laughter. I hear the pound of running feet. "Look!" she exclaims and then is still. Her sandals grate in the stone dust. "Feel what the neighbor gave to me." She is excited. Her words, her voice are laughing. "Feel."

I drop the chisel.

"Hold out your hands."

I feel something soft, trembling. The moist snuffle of snout, toes sharp as rice grains trouble my palm. The tail whips and wraps itself about my wrist.

"Imagine. Its fur is the color of toasted grain. The underside a pearly ivory. And the ears! Pink! If you hold it to the sunlight, you can see the tiny veins. . . . He was mowing. He scythed the nest. Only this one was left."

Sometimes, when I am lying still, I think of Maya, Durga, of my sons, and all the others: Gupta, and all his sixteen sons. I see us walking in a field. And the day is fresh, the air still powdery with dew. The mowers are advancing through the grass. Like waves of wind gathering speed, the grain bows before them.

We begin to run, one by one, until all of us are running. Some begin to fall or stumble. And all the while, the scythes move closer, ever closer, humbling the grass. . . .

 I LET MY hand run above the wattling, testing the darkness. I came upon what I knew was hidden there. Stones, these, not coin. They lay nestled in the carrying cloth. Even now, if I hoard anything, it is these. For from them I learned more than from any master.

I ran my thumbs over their contours. If it could, my gaze would probe beneath their surfaces still now, tracing the angle of the veins' incline, conjuring the forms, the fractures that lie hidden, wrapped in years of mystery like a child unborn lying in its mother's womb, its fingers scratching faintly at the ice.

I am unsure at what age I began collecting them, but I remember the occasion well enough: the stonecutter squatting on the rock pile that time, filling the folds of his *dhoti*.

"What are you doing there, old man? Isn't it enough to dress the stone all day without gathering these broken fragments in the night?"

He turned his turtle's face toward me. His eyes narrowed as he tried to read my features against the setting rays of sunlight. "Dressing comes only afterward. See here. This is where it all begins." He put the rock to his lips and spat on it, rubbing in the moisture with his fist. And handing me the stone: "There. Do you see?" Even in the half-light, it had become transformed, as though each grain, each small particle, although darker now, was lit from within. Without realizing, I crouched next to him. "Or this." He raised another stone to his lips before handing it to me.

"You are a carver, yes? Suppose that instead of tracing the outlines of the figures you are meant to set in stone, you let the stone tell you. What secrets, what marvels, what gods still lie hidden, trapped inside!"

I laughed. "I have been apprenticed these six years with the same master. But never has he told me to look inside the stone. It is not done that way. Impossible!"

He smiled at me slyly. "I *know* what is impossible. *You* are the one who asked the question." He raised his fist toward me as I stood up, impatient to be gone. Almost before I became aware, he had dropped a stone into my palm. "Now be off with you before your rice grows cold."

Only later did its weight remind me of what I had dropped without thinking in the fold of my *dhoti*. I pulled it from its hiding place. I spat on it as he had shown me. I held it to the light. Even then in the obscurity, it spread its colors, spilled them over the surface as oil spills on water. For a long time I studied it. Sometimes I saw winged warriors, sometimes chariots, and sometimes fierce angels, their swords raised, before the light failed and I slept.

 "AN HONOR, surely," said Gupta as we picked our way over the rock pile toward the roadway below. The Chola's wagon stood waiting for me. I had watched it in procession a thousand times, but that day I saw its splendor in a way I had not seen before. The driver sat in the shade of the overhang, waiting. Already the heat made the roadway shimmer although the morning was still young.

"You will be there by noon," promised Gupta, referring to the heat. "At the very latest." Then he blessed me, he who had opened his household to receive me when my own stood empty. "God be at your right hand —and everywhere else, my son." We embraced one another. I vaulted over the footrest.

The carriage was deep and shaded. It rode high above the road dust. The whip cracked over the twin rumps of the horses, sending up a cloud of flies. We lurched forward.

"Sail with a wind that is brisk," he called to me. I watched until his stooped figure had all but disappeared, still waving to me in the dust.

MAIN STAIRCASE (SOUTH SIDE)

 EVEN IN THE dreaming of it, the scene is curiously satisfying: they are unrolling the road. Behind me stretch the leagues and leagues I have traveled from the beginning, from the time I was first apprenticed, moving from one site to another, first with my fellows, carvers like myself, then with our cart, Maya, Durga, and my sons. They unroll huge bales of turf like sod before me, as they unroll the carpet for the palace guest, must still far to the east—where the new kings, the Sanjayas, have raised their capital.

As I lie waking, I have a sense of warmth, of pleasure, as if already I lay in sunlight, but the hesitating song of bird tells me it is not quite dawn. Blankets of turf, dull color of earth, of grasses long dry, matted together like felt—rolls and rolls of it. No matter how fast they unravel, there is still more, until at last it is high noon and I stand in the bleaching light of the harbor, waiting.

A tiny laugh laps at the shore of my waking and takes me bubbling in its wake: *Is there no one here to unroll the sea?*

 "IT IS NOT YET DAWN and already you are laughing." Her voice comes to me from the stepladder of the small enclosed pavilion in which we sleep. "I have brought you tea. The dawn air is always chilly."

"Do you never sleep?" I ask.

"Like a stone, now your hammer no longer wakes me in the night."

What she says is so. It has been still these nights, as if of late my days are spent in such dreaming that the night is blank, reprieved of dreams. Or, if I am visited, I am untroubled by them, dreams playful as the waves, and I fly or float, it matters little.

"There is in you something different," she observes quietly as she takes her leave.

"How different?"

" 'As if the lion ceased his hunting and stood still, as if the jackal slept.' "

Sometimes what she says sets something astir within me, as if while the days passed softly, rounding the corners of twilight, within me a giant slept. Then of a sudden, it is awake, prowling through the country of my waking, inhabiting my nights with dreams, a giant that is of me but not mine.

How can she know it? Does she read something in my face perhaps? I call to mind the look of blind men I have seen. What is that smiling *slackness* in the face? As if the shell that held them separate broke to admit a sunlight more burning than we seeing ones could know.

 "YOU WILL EXCUSE my poor attempts to speak your tongue?" Gunadharma has no need of apology. Despite a certain formality, his mastery is flawless. "I am not as fluent as I should be if I were acquainted with your country."

"Then how is it . . . ?" But the sun's rays force me to shield my eyes.

"Translations. You must know that in our monasteries here, we copy and translate the sacred texts."

"Karto!" He summons the fellow who squats outside waiting on the topmost stair, his brown feet splayed and caked with country mud. "So you may know the scheme of things well before our tour of the site tomorrow, I have arranged a visit for you of the wayside shrines which mark the route of pilgrimage. It will allow you a feeling of the countryside. Certain tasks disallow my going with you myself today. But the chief builder (he uses our word *takshaka*) will let you use his cart. The assistant here will show you the way."

The road takes us through a meadow green and hazy

with morning mist. But by the time we approach the main temple courtyard, the morning is already well advanced. The assistant helps me from the cart, which is really no better than a country wagon.

"Mendut," he points. Within the courtyard a series of curious domed structures squats row upon row. They look like nothing so much as giant chessmen plotted on a board. We circle them halfheartedly before making our way toward the temple and its welcome shade.

It is there in the corner, almost hidden to view, where the stair joins the molding of the basement, I catch sight of a panel truly of surpassing skill. A lion gazes at his reflection in a well. A jackal bides his time in the brambles, watching.

My guide approaches. "Sailendra," he points to the lion preening. I wonder is the lion emblem of the mighty Kedu dynasts. "Sailendra," he repeats, but his meaning stays closed to me. I do not know his language.

A knot of alms seekers crowds the entryway, demanding tribute of all who enter. At the foot of the stair, a solitary young man crouches, palm outstretched. To my surprise, the assistant—who must earn the wages of the meanest worker—leaves my side to slip him a coin. It is then I notice the sockets of his eyes gape empty. For the young man is blind.

 GUNADHARMA lets the scroll flutter open. I watch the subtle working of his fingers as he spreads it on the mat. "This text," he explains, smiling. "This Lalitavistara, for instance, is my hand."

"You serve both as scribe and master architect (I use our word, *sthapati*) and in one single lifetime?"

"Here in Kedu, we work at many tasks, where and as our abbot bids us. But only a monk such as myself is schooled to build a shrine."

He smoothes the scroll as it lies unfolded on the mat. "I have marked out for you each event to be depicted. You will see there are one hundred twenty of them— scenes to be carved—exactly the number of stone panels allotted to the cycle. . . . Do you have players?"

His question takes me by surprise.

"Players? In my country? Yes. I have seen them from time to time. *Yakshana.* They act out stories of the people."

"*Yakshana?* Here we have shadows, *wayan,* we call it. You and I are *wayan.* So the Lord Buddha (he refers to the Holy One). All, all is but shadow, a play of shadow figures against a screen of light. While the lamp shines we can be said to live—making war—or song; we dance briefly against the screen—until the darkness. So, too, the Lord Buddha. For you must know—although you yourself are Shivite—you must know that this Lalistavistara means 'the story of the play.' For it can be said the Lord Buddha only *performs* his incarnation into the shadow world of maya. He *assumes* his role of teacher. He is not obliged. For being Bodhisattva, he is sprung from the wheel of all desires."

My smile is inward. I am thinking: how is it that this monk, a chief *sthapati,* lends belief to such quaint notions? Are they not circuitous, do they not appear foolish, especially to us whose gods are engaged, as we, in the pull of being, at once weaving and tearing at the web, as wind and water tear, obedient to no law lesser than themselves?

I say nothing. I watch the dextrous play of fingers as he takes up the scroll fold by fold. "Study this well. Ask me what questions come to mind. I will try my best to answer."

 THE SCROLL is written in their curiously spare lettering. Despite the tilting slant of the characters, I read it well enough. The body of the text is copied in black, with this exception: that red ink illuminates the start of each new episode. I begin with the first illumination. I read:

According to the blessings of our great lord, and following his sacred teachings, the Life of the Holy One, Sakyamuni, he who was, is and will be forever Bodhisattva, Siddhartha Gautama.

The language is not difficult. Clearly this is but the introduction. I unfold the scroll till it stretches far into the shadows. Impossible to distinguish red from black in the obscurity. I slide the oil lamp along the matting. I read:

When his Mother, Queen Maya, felt her time approach, she had her servants convey her to the immense gardens called Lumbini. There, as she slept, she had a dream. . . .

Thus begins the story. Already it is not unknown to

me, for there are many who offer to the Holy One in our country. Leaving the scroll open on the ground, I move the oil lamp slowly, noting the illuminations as I go. There are one hundred and twenty as I finally assure myself when, in the darkest hour of the night, sleepless still with excitement, I read:

Through the night he prayed until the darkest hour when his disciples began to question him. When they had discoursed in this manner for some time, the dawn began to break. "Know, O my brothers," he began to preach, "this life is pain. . . ."

I blow out the lamp. I stretch out on the mat. I shut my eyes. Slowly they begin to take shape before me: the great procession, the Holy One waiting, impatient to be born, as I have waited these many years, darkness into light, to emerge at last, the carriage harnessed, the spokes of the great wheels, circles of fire striking sparks from the stone. The Coming set in motion. A Queen— Maya—reclining on the softness of stone cushions, her sleep swollen with dreams. . . .

 GUNADHARMA SHAKES me awake. He sets a bowl of steaming gruel on my mat.

"Be quick," urges this master among masters. "The cart is waiting."

Thirty monsoons—and more—have passed, but of that morning, I remember all: the particular clouds of moisture trapped in the steamy hammocks of the jungle, our passage through the rough terrain, and all along the river-course men laboring since dawn, struggling to wedge the boulders, to drive them up the riverbanks. Or crouching in the stream bed rough dressing the stone, squaring it in blocks. Stripped to the waist, women gather the slag, broken fragments of stone or rock. They struggle to raise their loads, poising them in towering balance on their heads. They move slowly, looking neither right nor left, barefoot along the river's edge. Others carry the loads beyond the jungle clearing, across the lush green meadow bordering the river and upward toward the site.

Then abruptly the palm groves thin. The shrine looms before us, a mountain among mountains. Never have I seen its like. It commands a valley edged by boiling lava flows, peaks which, even now, in the early morning haze, trail plumes of steam high above the clouds. The sky is heavy with them.

"Our country women are unrelenting." Gunadharma points to them with satisfaction. "They work tirelessly all day moving the slag, depositing it at the summit, slowly building up the mound."

"A perfect site! The bordering river, the mound set as if by design . . ."

"As if! The mound—like everything else—is made by men, every clod, every pebble, every stone was carried there to make it. And once the great blocks have been floated down the river and collected in the building sheds in sufficient numbers, there are plans to divert the river's course. The entire shrine will appear to float— a mirror of the universe!"

 THE CART LEAVES us at the foot of the eastern stair. At its base, a towering rock pile rises. Women load the stone and rock fragments into baskets that they pass from head to head down the steep incline, toward the stairwell.

Gunadharma steers me by the elbow. A gang of plasterers and painters are at work on the friezes that decorate the basement. At the farthest limit of the molding (and probably beyond the corner and lost to view), polychromists apply the black and red and green over the smooth white surfaces readied by the plasterers. Closer to us, a group of plasterers covers the bare stone reliefs with coats of calcium prepared and applied wet in such a way that it will bond with the fresh coat of paint.

A tall figure approaches us. "Here is the superinten-dent." (Gunadharma uses our word, *vardhakin*, to sig-nify he directs painting and plastering only.) Ketutengan is taller than most of his fellow islanders. He has an inward look, preoccupied. His right eye shows red and appears to smart. Repeatedly, almost spasmodically, he presses it shut. They exchange few words in their unknown tongue.

"The *vardhakin* promises to assign you a whitewashing apprentice," Gunadharma assures me.

What need have I of whitewash, I wonder. All along, Shanggal's promise rings in my ear: "You will supervise the carvers working under you. You will have full rein. One hundred, two hundred, on a project of such magnitude. . . ."

Idly, I study a panel lying partly obscured in the *vardhakin*'s shadow. It shows some naked figures steaming in a cauldron. Flames shoot upward about its base. The damned leap about in the fury of the fire's heat. Alongside, in mountains piled high as sweet cakes, hunters spear small animals. Perched on a high tor, an archer aims his arrow at a deer.

"A clever scheme to break the wide expanse": I point to the panel now it is no longer obscured by the *vardhakin*'s shadow, ". . . two representations side by side, yet unrelated one to the other. . . ."

Gunadharma smiles with a trace of condescension. "On the contrary. Those who fish or eat the meat of animals shall be cooked or roasted in hellfire as is their lot. For so we believe. The panels are far from unrelated. All along the basement here you can observe such scenes, all representations from our sacred texts, the Karmavibhangga or Jatakamala, all stories of evil punished—or of good rewarded."

We watch the *vardhakin* retreat along the line of

workers. He carries a bamboo reed that he uses inter-
changeably to point a detail or now and again to flog an
idler. At the base of the stair, stonecutters are at work
fitting the risers. Their hammers make the stone blocks
ring. A yet steeper stairway reaches sharply upward,
past the roughed-in galleries. As far as the eye can see,
gangs of women pass up basketloads of rock the distance
to the summit. We sidle past them in the narrow confine
of the stairwell. The smell of women's sweat contracts
my nostrils.

Along the first gallery, cutters are everywhere at
work, boasting the capstones which will be set to support
the finials of the balustrade. The walkway is littered with
calipers, mallets, and chisels. The cutters squat in whatever shade the unfinished balustrade can offer. Broken
rock litters the passageway. Gunadharma salutes the
workers only briefly. He conducts me to the inner wall.
The blackened stone is dressed and waiting. Each panel
is the width of my armspan, the height from my waist
to my highest reach.

"It is along here you will begin your work, starting
with this panel flanking the eastern gate, and working
always to your left."

My first thought is to break each panel by some
skilled device. But it is as if he reads my mind.

"To give each subject its proper due, you must take
up the breadth of the entire panel."

I will have to find some way to fill such vast expanse,
invent extra personages, whole orchestras, where one or
two musicians might have done. But that is nothing. It

is the piled-up courses of stone that daunt me, four in
all. I will have to plot the faces so as to avoid the cracks.
The lines of sand and lime mortar leave me little lati-
tude.

I run my finger along a seam. "Is each panel as I
see?"

"All one hundred twenty of them, all four courses
deep." He claps the stone dust from his hands.

We take the direction toward the south corner. I
notice the lower panels are already worked. I ask about
them.

"They picture the story of Prince Sudhana, who falls
in love with the elusive nymph Manohara."

"Curious to find the Manohara here in a gallery
given to the Bodhisattva," I remark.

"Not so. It celebrates the Sailendra founder, the
prince we called Sudhana, whose throne passed to his
son, our present king. The Manohara legend alludes to
his special love of truth. You remember the story? The
Manohara is a divine being. Only truth can capture her."

"I seem to remember that she could be caught only
by the hunter's snare."

"So the Sanskrit version has it. But with us, there
is no cruelty. That is why here the hunter sits as you see,
hands resting idly in his lap. He traps her with pure
truth, saying: 'If you be the nymph Manohara, daughter
of King Druma, stand still!' She of course complies!"

"An ingenious strategy," I say laughing.

Gunadharma falls silent.

We round the southeast corner. My eye follows the

progress of the story. But as we near the south gate, the friezes cease abruptly. Both upper and lower panels stand empty.

"What happened?" I ask dismayed.

"Oh, the story is ended!"

"And the carver?"

"The carver?"

"The one who made them?"

"Yes. They are beautiful."

"What happened to him?"

"He is gone."

Then I do not wonder at his curt reply. Carvers come and go. I am only impatient to begin my work.

**WE SIP TEA** in Gunadharma's hut at some distance from the site.

"I show you the master plans so that you may be seized with understanding. Our world is three, so is our temple three: shrine, stupa, and cosmos." His fine-boned hand sweeps across the Chinese paper. "Here, the sphere of desire (where we saw the figures of good and evil that decorate the basement); here, the sphere of form—but form free of desire (the four galleries, of which yours is the first, given to the lives of the Bodhisattvas in all their incarnations); and surmounting all, the world where being and nothingness collide, beyond form, beyond appearance, beyond all desiring." His fingers span three rungs of shrines shaped like temple bells rising ever more steeply toward a central shrine that crowns the summit, more vast than any of the others.

"Earlier today, you saw the stonecutters at work fitting the stairs, facing the upper galleries. But the top section as you see it here is not yet begun. It is nothing more than a growing pile of slag gathered from the riverbed, a desert, you might say, swept clean as any mountain peak. Yet when it is complete, each shrine will conceal behind its stone latticework the image of the Holy One spinning the wheel of law. But no one will be able to see it without first peering through the stone that veils it. And here," he indicates the crowning shrine, "an image of the Holy One, his hand raised in blessing, will be sealed for all eternity, left unfinished." He begins to recite from the closing words of the Lalitavistara: "Through the night he prayed until the darkest hour when his disciples began to question him. When they had discoursed in this manner for some time, the dawn began to break. 'Know, O my brothers, this life is pain.' "

Gunadharma sits quietly for some time. At last he turns the silence. "That is the great secret which no one, not the ordinary visitor, not even one of the ten thousand common workmen, not even the master artisans will ever know. I tell you—a foreigner—only because it has some bearing on your work. For your frieze ends—not with the death of the Holy One—but with the moment where he sits hand raised in blessing before the sermon can begin."

AFTER ALL THIS time, I wonder how the notion ever came to me that he was dull, this Karto. Perhaps from that first morning when the *vardhakin* assigned him to me as my whitewashing apprentice.

I fail to notice him at first, absorbed as I am in studying Gunadharma's scroll. I read aloud: "The Bodhisattva is in his heaven . . . *Tushita!*" (It is the word they use for 'heaven' in this tongue considered monkish here, although at home it is my daily practice.) I look up to find Karto, paint and brush at the ready. I am altogether unaware it is he who was my guide of yesterday. All these small brown men look alike to me. "Tushita," I repeat. He continues to stare at me. A dull fellow, surely, above and beyond our obvious difficulty: he knows nothing more of my tongue than a jungle parrot. I point to the word as it appears on the scroll. Carefully, he sets brush and paintpot down on the newly dressed flags of the terrace. His rough brown hands take the scroll from me. The better to see, he turns it upside down. This fellow has no reading! I look about for someone to help. The cutters squat, busy unrolling their carrying cloths. It is useless. None reads this language, none speaks it. I turn once more to this lumpen paintpot fellow. "Tushita," I shout. I spell the word. He stares at me dumbly. Then, quite simply, he hands me the brush. With his innocent gesture, he has made me an honorary brother of the painters' brotherhood! Abashed at my outburst, my feelings give way to amusement. I cannot explain to him why it is that I am laughing. I trace the letters on the molding above the panel. It will prompt my memory when the time comes to begin the drawings.

We continue our progress along the terrace, he carrying brush and paint in one hand, Gunadharma's scroll in the other. At each panel, I fasten upon a word or words to key my memory. I scrawl the letters above one panel following another until at last we turn the southeast corner. Already the sun beats on the blackness of the stone. We will have to hurry for I have in mind to reach the southwest corner in time to find some welcome moments of remaining shade. We work steadily, approaching the southern stair. I read aloud: "Seven days following the Bodhisattva's birth, his mother, Queen Maya, lies dying . . ." The heat is overwhelming. *"Queen Maya . . ."* I have lost the place. *". . . Seven days following the birth . . ."* Could it be sweat that makes the terrace swim? The painter eyes me expectantly. He makes to hand me the brush.

"No," I say. "Let us rest."

He looks at me dumbly. I touch his shoulder, invit-

ing him into the shadow of the south stairwell. The stone
canopy is not yet raised, but the verticals provide some
welcome shade. I take out my water gourd. I offer him
a sip. I watch him drink. Could it be this was my guide
of yesterday? We sit quietly for some moments. An
impulse takes me. I point to myself. "Gopal," I say. He
points to himself. "Karto," he says. It is then I know:
it is my guide of yesterday. I point to the stone. I say
the word in my tongue. Instantly he replies in his. So we
begin our conversation.

"Come!" I urge him. Quite suddenly his eyes light
up. He lifts the paintpot and brush and scampers down
the stairs in close pursuit. Rapidly we retrace our steps
eastward along the terrace, threading our way among the
cutters, sidestepping the scattered tools and capstones.
We round the corner moving back toward the east gate
to where the coolie women struggle over the rock pile.
Just beyond the teeming stairs, I find the corresponding
end panel. I cast a quick eye to the right and left to
assure myself: the panels are identically spaced. I re-
verse the scroll searching for Gunadharma's final indica-
tion. I read: "Through the night he prayed until the
dawn. . . ."

"Light," I decide without reading any further.

I look to Karto. His eyes search my face without any
understanding.

There are fifteen panels leading to the northeast
corner. We round it at last, close to the hour of the

brightest sun. In the shade of the corner niche we col-
lapse on the molding, laughing. For this reprieve is what
I sought. I hand Karto the gourd. He tips it to his mouth.
We give reckless reign to our thirst knowing that by this
stratagem of working backward, we will find shelter
through the hottest portion of the day.

Past the north gate toward the northwest corner, I
read: "The Bodhisattva takes the path to the river where
he is bathed by celestial beings." Once more it comes to
me. I see the water, its surface rocking against the rim,
a bowl of light. *Trap it,* she whispers, *make it shimmer
in the stone. See how you would trap it.*

The air all around seems to pulse without moving.
Already I see the scene take shape. I know within certainty: it is here I will begin; it will bring luck. Once
more I see the Chola wheel his horse. "Krishna," I
whisper. I look to Karto. He appears not to have heard
me. In any case, in my tongue, the names of gods are
all the same to him.

The sky reddens with approaching sunset as we turn
the southwest corner. There are fifteen panels more till
we reach the completion point at the near side of the
southern gate. Will daylight last us until then? Already
making out the text has become difficult. Along the
terrace, the cutters are noisily shouting to one another,
rolling up their tools in the carrying cloths. We must
sidle past the great stone blocks if we are to come close
enough to the panels to paint their names. At last, ex-

hausted, shaken by the hubbub, we reach the south gate.
The sky has turned blood red. I hold the scroll up to the
light. In the fiery reflection I read: "An aged seer fore-
tells the prince will become Buddha. Then falling down,
he weeps: his ears will be too stopped to hear the Buddha's teaching."

"Blind!" The word is on my lips before I know it.
Why did I say it, I wonder, when it was deaf I meant?
A stillness reigns over everything, a kind of peace. The
ring of the chisels still haunts the air with its particular
absence. The night breeze lifts its whispering in the
hammocks of the jungle. The palm fronds crackle gently
in its soft embrace. I look to where Karto is standing.
But he has vanished with the others. The gallery is
deserted. And on the flagstones the paintpot stands
where he set it down, its brush poking straight upward
in the shadows.

 THE SKY SWELLS, IMMENSE and lavender with sunset. Here and there, high in its vault, a lone bird makes its way home. I watch the beating of its wings, golden in last light.

Blind. Why did it come to me? I close my eyes. The sound of evening is clear, distinct. The cry of birds, the susurrus of palms in the groves, the call of some animal, far in the jungle. Now I open them and hold my ears. Which would I prefer? It is a question. To not be able to see this splendor? Or to be able to see and not hear it? (Or perhaps by hearing, see?) But no. I am a carver. I have need of seeing. I try to imagine working without the drum of chisels all around me, the clink, clink, the brittle syncopation of a thousand cutters at work. I shut my eyes. Wheels of fire strike sparks into the stone.

I do not hear the footsteps at first, perhaps because my eyes are closed, my ears tuned to some inner drumming. They stand below me on the terrace. I am struck by their stance, feet spread apart, arms akimbo. One of them speaks to me. Clearly he asks me something. I

stare at him blankly. My ears still hum. Now he is
shouting. I turn my palms outward to show I understand
nothing, that I am unarmed. It is a signal for them. They
grasp my arms and jerk me to my feet. Gunadharma's
scroll goes clattering down the stairs. They do not stop
to pick it up. After a brief exchange of words among
themselves, they march me to the western gate and down
the stairs into the twilight.

As we near the supervisors' compound, we veer to
the right. In the distance I can distinguish long rows of
sheds, pavilions where even now people are sitting eating by lamplight or unrolling matting, temporary shel-
ters for the workmen, probably. At last we mount the
steps of a hut. The bamboo shade is lifted and we enter.
They still hold me fast, one to each side, clamped at the
armpits. Words are exchanged with a man who appears
to give them orders. He waves a pudgy hand, brushing
them away. They release me from their grasp. I am
aware of some tingling in my arms and in the palms of
my hands. He says some words to them. Then, turning
to me, in Sanskrit he says: "They are not to touch you.
You are one of ours."

One of ours, one of theirs, clearly there is a difference.
Where, I wonder, does the distinction lie?

"I am Gopal, the carver in stone," I say.

"Sastri," the fat man says, saluting me. "And they
(with a casual sweep of the hand in their direction) are
the Sailendra fellows. They guard the site from intruders
—and they guard intruders from the site."

"Isn't it the same?"

"Only sometimes." His giggle is high-pitched. He wheezes for breath.

So this is Sastri, the carving superintendent, the chief *takshaka* to whom I myself am answerable. His was the cart Gunadharma borrowed to take us to the site. Now he invites me to sit.

"Let us take our ease." He offers me some mandris and honey.

"I am worried," I say. "I left Gunadharma's scroll at the site. Perhaps it would be better if I were to return for it."

"Just for a moment." I watch him peel the heavy purple rind. "Let us take our ease. And then I myself will accompany you." The fruit lies in his fleshy palm, white and sectioned. "There is never anyone on the site after sundown." He throws a look over his shoulder at the men who even now slouch against the roof posts. "They see to that," he says, amused. "The scroll will be where and as you left it."

We make our way by lamplight in the darkness. For one of his girth, Sastri moves rapidly through the palm groves. Only his labored breathing gives him away. The darkness hangs over us like a pall. The moon has not yet risen. We talk in whispers.

"They allow no one on the terraces after sundown. They took you for a troublemaker."

"Even sitting? calmly at peace? studying the sunset?"

"You are a stranger." We mount the western stairs in silence. "Where did you leave it?" His question cuts short my reverie.

"It fell. They would not let me stop to take it."

"Which gate? Do you remember?"

"I am not sure," I lie. My hope is to be left alone.

"Take the lamp yourself. I will wait here for you."

One by one the stars pierce the pall of darkness, dangling like the jewels of Indra's net. The night is warm, sweet scented. The air hovers soft, like the trembling wings of dragonflies.

I round the corner to the east. The moon has risen. It lifts above the treetops, bathing the stone in pewter light. Mist crowns the hammocks of the jungle in a steamy nimbus. Lost to Sastri's view, I let the lamp go out. By moonlight, the stone takes on an aspect I could not have imagined, silent, secret, as though forms slumbered deep beneath the surface, waiting even now for someone to quicken them.

I continue past the southern gate before remembering why it is I came: I stop short to retrace my steps. In the moonlight, I find the paintpot where Karto abandoned it. The scroll lies where it fell.

 WHY DID I CHOOSE to work on it first, far beyond the midpoint of the cycle, beyond the north gate, this scene of the Holy One bathing? To some, it would have seemed more reasonable to start at the beginning, but I . . . Perhaps it reminded me of that time following hard on my apprenticeship, that scene of the Lord Krishna bathing in the stream, the slight and poignant turn of the young limbs courting the sunlight.

I examine the stones, looking for fault marks. With a small brush made of animal hairs, I sweep the surface clean of dust. I study the joinings. Quickly I begin to sketch the lines using the charcoal stick, erasing with palm or elbow if I am not satisfied.

Already this scene is "in the eyes," for each morning I wake before sunup. I lie on the mat eyes closed or open —it matters little—letting my spirit wander, apparently aimlessly. Then, in such reverie, it comes to me. I know what it is that I must do. In this I am guided by the *silpasastra,* for there is no reason here for the Bodhisattva to find himself anywhere but at the center.

With the charcoal stick I position head and nimbus clear of the joining. Below, I form the torso, curving ever so gently so that it occupies the third course of stone; the legs, one knee very slightly bent, occupy the second; the feet are planted on a lotus cushion, one somewhat forward, poised on the very molding that borders the panel —but this is subtle illusion. I will have to incise and work the stone with my utmost skill to make it thus appear.

In the riverbed, I sketch the small fry frolicking in the stream, wavelets, water plants. I group three heavenly attendants filling their conches in the stream bed, and above, flying on a cloud bank, divine attendants offering sweet scented garlands. I step back, immensely satisfied, for in the shallow span of four courses I have fit two rows of figures, yet they appear comfortably uncrowded. I fill in mountains to the right. Here the *silpasastra* is reassuringly explicit: hills are to be storied, capped by rounded summits. At the base I coil a connubial pair of water serpents, friends of the Bodhisattva, perhaps, from a previous life.

The fog has lifted. My efforts have taken the better part of the morning. I sit on the molding, resting, drinking water from the gourd. Even the air seems to gasp for breath at this hour. The sounds of chisels at work on the south side drift toward me on the jungle air. It occurs to me that all the while I worked at fever heat, somehow I had not heard or noticed their insistent syncopation.

I replace my gourd. I remove paint and brush from my roll. I prepare to fix these charcoal lines with paint

which neither wind nor weather can erase until such
time as I am ready for the incising chisel. The *vardhakin*,
occupied below on the north basement, catches sight of
me at work with the brush. I see him approach as I stand
wiping my brow. He makes signs to me—he does not
speak my language. He gestures "painting," points in
the distance. I fail to grasp his meaning. Then he catches
sight of someone on the tier above. There is much shouting. I see Karto come running along the gallery.

The *vardhakin* points to my brush, my paint. Instantly Karto seizes them from me. It is useless to protest. Neither speaks my language. I am used to my own
painting, prefer it, for I have learned to couch in it
signals which will remind me later, when my chisel has
need of them, what it was that I intended. Karto cocks
his head, studying the charcoal sketch. He smiles at me
approvingly. He begins carefully to apply the paint. We
are alone. I watch him.

"Thus," I say, taking up the brush once more. I
broaden the line, now narrow it by twisting the bristles
this way or that or by changing the slant. He casts a
quick eye at me to show he understands. To emphasize,
I take up the charcoal, reinforcing the shadow effect I
desire. At once he nods his understanding. Where had
the idea ever come to me that he was simple?

"Brush," I say.

He replies in his language. I repeat. He corrects.

"Paint," I say. Again he replies. We continue in this
way for some time, I sketching rapidly in charcoal from
the word we have traced above each panel, he fixing the

lines with quick and skillful brush strokes. We talk as we work. I learn to say plain things, to ask for simple wants.

We have been at our task for many days when the *vardhakin* chances upon us still at work in the north gallery. I am sketching a tree, Karto watches.

"Branch," I say. "Trunk."

But the *vardhakin* interrupts. He says something sharp to Karto. Karto throws me a glance. His eyes grow troubled. The *vardhakin* raises his voice.

"What is the matter?" I ask.

"He says that carving is a prayerful act. He wants no talking here."

Karto signifies "talking" by using the word for his language. Much later, after the *vardhakin* takes his leave, I whisper to Karto: "Then let us have Sanskrit talking here!"

 IT WAS NOT this way closer to home. As the weeks pass, I try to discover what sense there is in their way of doing things: no organization apparently save the obvious one: a hierarchy of master builder and priest; and beneath them, tiers of functionaries, as immovable as the temple itself, constant interference by officials who know *nothing*! And the cutters, carvers, surveyors, painters—swarms of them—ten thousand, Gunadharma claims. Yet where are they all? Where do they come from? And who pays? Who guarantees their *kalam* of rice? The Sailendra? Yet they make no wars, as do the Chola, to restock empty coffers. . . .

We are at work. "Karto," I ask, "how much?"

"Of what?"

I extract a coin from my *dhoti.*

"Money," he says.

I repeat, "How much?"

We do this for some time. I gesture. I tap his palm. We struggle for the meaning for I forget the word for 'wages.'

"No, no!" he exclaims at last. "No wages! There is
no money for it!"

"None of you work for wages here? No one is paid?"

"No, no," he corrects me. *Vardhakin* is paid."

"And you? How much?"

"No. No wages."

"Only rice?"

"No, no. We must pay for rice."

"But the *vardhakin* works for wages."

"Yes. For wages and for rice."

 THE MONSOON SEASON approaches. The heat drives me to the north side by mid-morning at the latest. To work on the south terrace at all, we must begin shortly after dawn. My plan is to complete the drawings on all four sides in this manner, taking advantage of shifting light and temperature, before the incising can begin.

We make good progress. I have designed a special scaffold to ease my task. Strong enough to hold two men, it is cradled on a cross frame that can be raised or lowered at will, depending on the height at which I need to work. Karto adds another refinement: a white cloth canopy strung like a sail, which he keeps watered through the greatest heat.

A crowd of cutters gathers to watch us. Little by little other canopies spring up. Everywhere I notice there is talking and laughter. The *vardhakin* apparently hears nothing. Is it perhaps my particular talking that offers inconvenience? Later the thought comes to me: have they perhaps counted on my not speaking their language?

As we adjust the height this morning, I sense something unusual. But it is nothing I can pinpoint. Karto climbs the platform. "Have you observed? No women!"

It is true. The rock pile is deserted. The women are gone. The east stairs, normally choked with teams of women porters, are empty and silent. I hand him brush and paint.

"What do you think may be the reason?"

Karto shrugs. "Sooner or later, we will discover it. We must wait and see."

Sometime toward the height of the morning we begin to hear a shouting from the direction of the river. We continue with our charcoal and paint. But the cries assume an insistent rhythm hard to ignore. I pose my charcoal on the ledge. We cross the terrace to straddle the parapet. Far across the meadow we have an unobstructed view. The river carries a flotilla of wooden rafts made of logs lashed together. On these float the huge blocks which I immediately guess are intended to face the upper terraces. Crouched on the riverbank, porters dressed in loincloths wedge the blocks and snare them. At the far end of the meadow, long lines of porters heave on signal of their foremen, inching the blocks up the steep incline onto rows of logs already set level on the floor of the clearing. All around them, the women are at work stripping tree trunks bare, setting the rollers in place, laboring to extend the log beds across the meadow clear to the storage sheds. For these blocks are the weight of ten men and can be moved no other way.

Day to day, we follow their approach. Overseers

walk along the tracks of logs. Their rhythmic chanting continues to regulate the pace. We watch them struggle for some time before we take up our work high on our platform. But we can follow their progress by the sound of the chanting coming ever nearer until at last the front line of porters reaches the storage sheds far below where we work.

**FOR SOME DAYS,** I have not seen Gunadharma at the site. I wonder at it, true, but it never occurs to me something may be amiss. I have been at work some two days now, rough-drawing the panel that shows the Bodhisattva comforting his wife Gopa, who has awakened from bad dreams. From my vantage point in the western gallery, I can see the workers' compound stretching across the meadow almost as far as the eye can see. Each pavilion is of identical size; there is enough room in each to bed some fifty or sixty men, sleeping mat to mat. If each cooks his own rice? Yes, it could be done. . . . Some three thousand at most in this compound. But where are the others? Can they be scattered elsewhere: coolie women who struggle across the meadows from rock pile to rock pile, hauling baskets to the site, men squatting in the riverbed, rough handling the boulders, dressing the stone? And what of the quarry men? Could it be they account for several thousand more?

I have arranged the couple on a raised bed, shielded

from the view of their attendants by a canopy. Karto's absence delays the work. They have been queuing today since dawn. Each is assigned an hour to report, but notwithstanding this clumsy attempt at organization, the lines move slowly. Somewhere below Karto must await his turn.

I turn my attention back to the couple. Their faces press close to one another in their troubled night. It is all in the feeling of the eyes, the look with which each holds the other. The grace of their bodies is accented by the length of the platform on which they lie.

I drop the lines of the canopy past the base of the platform, entirely veiling the lovers in the privacy of their bed, so that their nakedness is hidden to all but one another. In the wide expanse to either side I begin to group female attendants, asleep, their rounded forms resting softly, against one another. They sleep with their mouths slightly open, heads thrown back.

Something is different, I am not sure what. I am too absorbed in the drawing to take much notice at first. A sudden shouting interrupts my trend of thought. I remember Karto. I rush to the parapet. There is a knot of men scuffling on the ground. A sea of backs writhes in the struggle; limbs flail. Almost immediately, the Sailendra guards come running from the supervisors' compound. They surround the combatants the better to seize them. One after another, they are dragged off. Some of them, still struggling, are clubbed into submission.

Karto returns running from the line-up.

"What happened?"

"The rice," he says, panting. "They have reduced each measure by nearly one-quarter."

"Is it that which caused the trouble?"

"Some cutter was at the root of it. He tried to collect twice, once for himself, once again for his brother. It was then the others jumped him."

We see the *vardhakin* approaching. Quickly we fall silent and resume our work.

 For some days now, we hear the chant of the overseers pacing the slow advance of the porters. Our first curiosity has given way. Yet it is as if the chant with its insistent rhythm in reality is meant for us, so impossible is it to ignore. The line continues to just before day's end, although by then we are at work on the north side, where it comes to us, if it comes at all, filtered by the heat of the jungle air.

We are preparing to move the scaffold. A shout calls us to the balustrade. Far below, a porter lies fallen. His anguished cries fill the heat-heavy air. His leg is partly crushed beneath a stone block. The overseer makes to raise the whip. A porter lets go the rope to shield his fellow porter from the lash. All the while the chant continues. Porters shoulder the ropes, several to a team, struggling to deposit the rough-cut blocks at the foot of the southern gate.

"They are weak," Karto whispers. "All along the line there has been trouble. Ever since the rations were cut. They have begun to feel it."

 I AM THE LAST THIS evening to receive my
ration. Sastri invites me inside his pa-
vilion. He is alone. The 'Sailendra fellows' are not in evidence.

"There has been some trouble lately. Nothing serious. But let me caution you. Be on your guard."

I fail to understand. "Is there something that is not
right in what I do?"

"No, no. Nothing like that. How shall I say? For
example, this measure of rice, where do you store it?"

"In my sleeping place. Why?"

"Out in the open?"

"No, inside. Since the monsoon."

"You must conceal it now. For your own good. A lost
ration cannot be replaced."

 "Is there much thieving?" Karto is puzzled at my question. "People taking things? Rice, for example?"

Karto turns serious. "I have not heard of any. But there is trouble."

"What kind of trouble?"

"In the villages soon it will be planting time again. The people here, some of them try to return to work their rice fields in the night. If they are caught . . ."

"What happens to them?"

"Here? Maybe just a flogging. But if they are caught in their villages . . ."

"Then what?"

"Then it goes badly with them. They are bound hand and foot, trussed on the carrying pole so that many of them hang face down. Porters take them to the quarry. They are forced to cut the stone."

"Where is the quarry?"

"Far. On the shoulder of Merapi, somewhere near the crater. No one knows exactly." He indicates the mountain, even now sending up its plume of steam. I guess it to be five days' walk from here.

 I FEEL MY WAY. Under my sleeping platform, there is an area, sunken from the rest, where dead leaves lie in the hollow of the ground. I wait for darkness. I know there will be no moon. The work of digging is slow, the ground, even here has dried. The hole must be deep to the elbow if it is to cover the jar. I work into the night until at last, I think it may be ready.

Back inside I grope for the jar in the darkness. What if, caught up in my digging, what if the very thing I hoped to forestall happened? What if someone crept in to take it while I sought to prepare its hiding place? My bowel drops: it is not there! Of course! Should I cry— or laugh?

But no, my fingers meet the jar's rough curve. It is there, recessed in the corner a little farther than I remember. I remove the lid, reach inside the rim. The grain falls, a hard rain slipping through my fingers. Enough here for a month!

Durga must have taught me well.

 I HAVE BEGUN work at the southeast corner, on the panel that shows Queen Maya journeying through the countryside.

"Karto," I ask him on an impulse, "tell me about your village." Karto interrupts his work with the brush.

"My village? It is like any other village."

"When you take the path through the village, what does your eye see there?"

Karto leans his head back and shuts his eyes. A smile unlike any I have seen before opens his face as sunlight passes through a rain cloud. "Oh," he sighs.

"What do you see?"

"The rice fields. . . . The path turns through the jungle. It straightens out, the vines and fern banks fall away, and there, almost as far as the eye can see, the rice fields lie in rows—for we live in the valley. It is a long way from there to the terraces which line the mountain."

"Can it be something like this?" I draw rapidly with the charcoal stick until a vast expanse of cultivated fields

stretches to the far distance. Karto stands looking over
my shoulder.

"It is exactly like." He trades some comment with
a stonecutter—perhaps from the same village—who
joins us watching. They comment in their tongue. "Exactly like," they agree. Another stonemason joins them.

"A road is no road without an oxcart." He points a
finger. I sketch the cart, the pair of buffalo, their sharp
horns lowered, struggling to pull their burden.

"And the sky, without a flight of ducks." The stonecutter points, I dot the sky with birds in flight.

"And my mother singing in the fields," says Karto,
"knee deep in water, planting." I place a figure stooping
in the foreground.

"She needs a hat, against the sun."

I am not sure what he means at first.

"A hat . . . like a basket. An umbrella made of
straw." He uses the shaft of his brush to draw a shape
in the dust. The masons laugh at my incomprehension.

I stand back. I see that what I have made without
any planning is a picture of this countryside, the way the
fields lie, the way the rows of planters—whole families
of them—stoop in the paddy fields.

But the laughter of the masons dies abruptly. The
vardhakin has appeared just below us on the terrace.

 TODAY IS CAUSE for celebration: the designs are complete at last. One hundred twenty panels ready and outlined in calcium paint. I have counted them. We expect Gunadharma today—or tomorrow perhaps. For before I can begin incising, he must pass on what is finished.

How can I have imagined that he would be alone? Already in the distance, it is clear: he is flanked to either side. Sastri and Ketutengan, the *vardhakin,* accompany him. The terrace has been cleared of all obstruction. They walk three abreast. They begin at the east gate, moving always to the left. I follow at some distance. I observe them point this way and that, but their voices are lost in competition with the steady ring of cutters' chisels in the upper galleries. They move slowly from one panel to the next without varying their pace. At the southeast corner, they halt abruptly. There is much pointing and gesturing. The *vardhakin,* especially, seems more animated, more insistent than usual. I wonder what it is that can have so engaged their attention.

Back at the east gate, Sastri and the *vardhakin* take their leave. Gunadharma bids me follow him. We walk silently in the direction of the southeast corner. Gunadharma stops once more opposite the fifteenth panel.

"What did you intend by this?" he asks.

"It is Queen Maya on her way . . ."

"I know the subject," he cuts me short. "What did you mean showing this countryside? . . . the rice . . . ?"

"There is no meaning. The Queen is described riding through the countryside."

"But why the rice?"

"No reason. It is the countryside. What more reason can there be?"

"To everything there is meaning. Nothing is accident. The fields, the planting have no place in the procession."

"Not in the procession. Of course. Only in the countryside it passes."

"Neither in the procession nor in the countryside. The background distracts the mind from the only meaning, the coming of the Holy One."

"Then you wish it changed . . . ?"

"Yes. It will be necessary. Only let Sastri know when you are finished."

 WE WORK IN the hot sun of the east side without respite. Karto applies abrasive to the surface. All the morning he struggles with the pumice stone. The lines of the distant hills slowly disappear, the dikes that line the rice fields, the formation of birds in flight, the bullock cart. At last all has vanished of the background but the row of planters hung in emptiness.

Karto stops work. The pumice stone shatters on the terrace floor. He has not simply paused to wipe his brow.

"Karto," I whisper, taking his arm. Quietly I walk him into the shade of the canopy that crowns the gate. In the three years we have worked together, I have never seen him weep. Tears set rivers in the stone dust on his face. He wipes his eyes with his forearm, but the stream does not stop.

"Karto." I stare at him dismayed. I am without any words of comfort. "This erasing is not my order."

He nods.

"Gunadharma ordered it."

He nods to show he understands.

"He could not know."

"He does not wish to know," he whispers.

"How could he know it was your village, your people there planting the rice?"

"My people." He nods darkly. "My people. Year after year we struggle for them here. This temple. This temple is none of our affair. We are farmers. It is we who plant the rice. We make the ground yield for them, season after season. Without rice, nothing happens: no life, no food, nothing that is beautiful. Only emptiness, emptiness as empty as that sky there, or that earth.

"Look," he whispers to me in altogether a different tone. "Look if anywhere here, in any of the hundred panels, you see rice anywhere but in the golden bowls of princes!"

 Karto applies the final strokes of paint. We work at close range to one another. I am ready to begin the incising. I start at the top so that the stone dust can fall free: there are no recesses below to catch it. I brush the surface as I go. It is the outlining chisel I use. As soon as the preliminary lines are complete, I will have assigned to me one, then two, or possibly even three more assistants, carvers like myself, who will begin the backgrounds under my watchful eyes. Karto will probably be sent to work in the next gallery where new reliefs are being designed.

The noon hour is quiet. The cutters' hammering is temporarily still. The *vardhakin* is nowhere in sight. We eat our cold rice sitting against the molding in the shade of the angle.

"Where did you learn painting, Karto?"

"Here. On the basement carvings in the courtyard."

"Then you were never apprenticed?"

"No! I am a farmer! All of us working here are farmers!" He seems very insistent.

"But you have been painting here for some time now?"

"Five monsoons. Soon to be six. They care only for building here. The rice is none of their affair."

"Then this rice they issue, where does it come from if not the villages?"

"The Sailendra. The Sailendra have it. Stored in their granaries. They have been claiming the large portion for themselves for many seasons."

"And now they issue it back to you."

"Oh, no! The overseer makes us mark each time."

"Who works your fields?"

"My mother. They did not take her. She is too old to carry."

"Take her?"

"Yes. The Sailendra men. They came one morning to the village before anyone was awake. They entered our compound. Others circled it so no one could escape. Then they forced us from our huts. 'You and you, and you there.' There was just time to take a carrying cloth with a handful of rice."

"And if you could not go?"

"You always go."

 I SET THE NEW assistant to work on the decorations. Can he have learned his carving in the rice fields, I wonder? I have all I can do to cool his wretched fervor. A garland here, a string of jewels there—my design becomes all noise with no silence in it.

"Here," I say, showing him. I exert my utmost patience to still my agitation. Sintal is his name. Sintal! How I miss Karto's quick smile of recognition.

I return to work the figures—stone angels, floating improbably on air, flying with no more weight in the substance of the stone than the light of morning. Even now I remember the heat, the longing, the throbbing in the eyes. The light.

 I SIT BROODING in the darkness. The small fire has lasted barely long enough to cook my rice. There will be little left for tomorrow—and that eaten cold—while I incise the figures of the marriage bed. I stare into the embers. How to coax the blackened stone to yield its secret? For how can those who come later—in sunlight—how can they be made to feel the darkness hold them in its spell? My attendants, their mouths agape in sleep, are shabby tricks at best.

The night breeze whispers in the palm fronds, the embers flicker.

"Gopal!" Maya's black hair spreads beside me on the pillow. "Gopal!" I watch her eyes grow wide. Her hand reaches in the darkness. "Gopal, I tremble." She holds my hand to her womb. "Here. In my emptiness."

 IN THE SOFT GRASS, footsteps startle me. But it is no ghost. Karto stands before me in the darkness. He is laughing.

"How did you come here?" I whisper.

"I escaped!"

"From the compound?" I am unbelieving.

"There is a way. Darkness befriends the thief and the plain woman!" Something about him troubles me.

"Eat," I urge him. I make room on the stone beside the waning fire. His refusal troubles me the more. "What is it?" I say.

"My mother has need of me for the planting. She has no one left."

I decide to hold my tongue. Better not to dwell on the risk. He settles his wrapping cloth onto his knees. He works the knots loose. "I want to leave you this," he says. "It may prove useful."

He frees a small carved gourd. He holds it close to the embers so I can better judge of its design.

"I, too, am a carver," he jokes.

"Is the work yours?"

"All mine. We make them in the village."

I examine it carefully.

"Do you know its use?" He takes it from my hands. The lid is cunningly fashioned so that at first its joining is not apparent. He opens it. In the darkness I see the pearly glow of something white. Dark fragments, apparently of dried leaves, rustle to the touch.

"Betel," he explains. "If you mix them, the nut with the powder—thus—it banishes hunger—and all thought of hunger. You may have need of it."

 THE *VARDHAKIN* comes to a stop. He stands quietly eyeing me for some time from below as I work on my platform. I have been expecting his visit.

At last: "This Karto. Have you seen him?"

"No. Seen him I have not. . . ." My uncertain command of his tongue deserts me momentarily. The *vardhakin* appraises me silently. "I thought he must work elsewhere, or with another."

"He is not with another. He is gone from the compound."

"I am sorry, I grew to depend on him," I say simply. It is the only true response left to me, for I am unwilling to feign surprise. Let them be caught up in their own difference: it is none of my affair.

"I thought you might know where."

There is something in his manner, as if he cannot quite decide does my apparent unconcern stem from utter ignorance, or do I mask what it is I know. Some inner malice prompts me: "If he comes, I will tell him that you seek him."

The *vardhakin* flashes me an angry look. His departing grunt signals my own sense of relief.

 STILL AT WORK in the western gallery where I deepen the figures of Gopa's dream, I catch sight of the women working. I watch for a time as they drive fence posts for a new compound. Who will occupy it, I wonder? Not the porters who even now continue landing the great blocks from the rafts along the river. Perhaps the women themselves. For then I had not yet learned that women were kept apart in a clearing far in the jungle, an hour's walk from the site.

Even in the soft haze of the afternoon light, I decide there is something gaunt and ragged about them, as if the dust of the compound had bleached out the bright color I remember of their dress. They work in silence, without talk or laughter.

Of Karto, there is no sign.

 THE SOUNDS OF the grappling hooks can be heard from early dawn. Even before the gateway arch becomes the lookout station for the overseers, it is clear: changes will come about now and swiftly. The women are dismantling the overseer's booths, pulling down the canopies. I catch sight of them from time to time, dragging the wattling to the new compound.

The booths no longer serve to distribute rice to the line-up. Now the *takshaka* sits at the head of the east gallery with the other overseers parceling out the rice by measure, pouring it into the sacking cloths. Along the gallery, the assistants move from one man to another. Each cutter marks his sign on the paymaster's ledger. Rice is doled out every fourteen days. At first I do not question it, for I am not affected. But now that age has made me wary, I am sure of it: for confined in the narrow expanse of the galleries, the cutters were far less prone to mass or to engage in violent squabbles.

When in the privacy of his hut where I have come to receive my own ration, I ask Sastri about the change, he claims this way it takes less time away from working. What I find interesting is what he fails to say: for although my ration remains the same, the common measure is reduced by almost half. Doled out every fortnight, it appears more generous. Yet, in fact, it is far less.

 THERE IS A MURMURING above the ring of chisels. Even at this distance Sastri's girth announces him. Following him, a quartet of Sailendra guards struts in stiff precision. At the far end of the gallery I see him pause to address them, pointing now this way, now that. Before I have time to speculate, the guards move swiftly toward a cutter squatting beneath a canopy. Even at this distance, the rip of cloth is unmistakable. What can they intend? They find another improvised overhang, and another, approaching along the gallery toward the corner where I am at work. Whatever the reason, it becomes clear to me: either I dismantle Karto's improvised shade, or lose it to the guards. I must be quick about it. I fumble with the ties in their grommets. I gather the sheeting in haphazard folds. I sit on it as on a pillow where at this height none will see it.

A small triumph in its way, perhaps. But my thought is only of the interruption, of my resentment at it.

 I CLIMB THE stairs toward the eastern gate, my tools wrapped in my carrying cloth along with rice and gourd. I am still gray with sleep. It is only as I raise my eyes at last that I see the strange bamboo construction dominating the gate's superstructure. For above it rests a platform surmounted by a still higher seat, raised as if on stilts. And over it, incongruously in this sunless dawn, a parasol.

I am the first to arrive. I determine to begin work on the east face this morning. I round the corner into the southern gallery in search of my platform. It is not where I left it. I stop to consider. I bring to mind last evening's sunset. Where had it found me? But, yes. The memory is clear. I had returned to the south side to finish what I had begun in the cool of early morning. But the platform is not here. I go circling the terrace in search of it. It is nowhere to be found. I return to the eastern gate. It will be difficult to work without it. I have grown accustomed to the comfort it offers. Then I see it at last: far below, it lies shattered, its frame broken, on the rock pile.

IT WILL NOT be long before the cutters begin arriving. Already I hear voices coming from below. I stamp my feet in the morning chill, untying the knots of my carrying cloth. It lies spread on the ledge. I remove the chisels, the mallet, the animal-hair brush. I lay them out where I can easily feel for them on the molding below. I retie the cloth and stow rice and gourd inside the angle of the wall.

Sastri's footsteps reach the level of the gallery. He is accompanied by two assistants. Is now the time to talk to him about my platform? Or should I choose my time more carefully? I am poised in my moment of indecision when he addresses me with a correct but distant greeting.

"Sastri!" I say. "It is you!" I approach along the gallery. He waits expectantly, saying nothing. "It seems my platform has been discarded by mistake . . ." But before I can continue, he interrupts: "It is no mistake. I ordered it."

"*Why?*" I cannot damp my tone of voice.

"I have been meaning to speak to you." He walks me out of his assistants' earshot. "You must realize that no shrine is built unless the people know they are to work—and *only* work. Unfortunately, they have grown slack. They seem to take their license where they find it—from your canopy, for instance. You saw. We put an end to that! From now on, all support structures will come by our order. And only by our order. We will design whatever we believe is needed. All the galleries will be worked from a builder's scaffold of uniform height. The work to assemble it will begin today. You will no longer have to drag your own from place to place. You may even circulate from frieze to frieze without having to touch the gallery floor!"

"But it will be stationary, incapable of being raised or lowered at will."

"Of course."

I make one last attempt. "Isn't it less costly to have a small platform that can be moved from panel to panel as the need requires?"

Sastri laughs. "The price of bamboo is cheap enough," he says, "and we have more than enough people willing to build it." We are back to the east gate now. He pauses, one foot already raised on the ladder leading to the platform. "Now if bamboo matched the cost of rice. . . ." He begins to mount the ladder.

**THE OTHER TERRACES** are cordoned off. From where he presides under his parasol, Sastri has taken full vantage. Under his direction, the assistants draw up lists of panels, of sections, of balusters, of finials, of niches to be completed on schedule. Each cutter, each carver must make his mark to show he understands.

I consider: is it perhaps that the Sailendra has given orders to quicken the pace? Is it perhaps his emptying granaries that prompt him?

"Sastri," I say, "I (and my assistants) can barely carve: the heat, the schedules, the restrictions, the scaffolds. . . . If there were perhaps a chance of moving freely. . . ."

"There is no chance. You must understand we are working with a deadline. Come the monsoon, this section must be finished."

But he has softened. For on the morrow we are met with a new improvement: on the platform sits a water carrier. His job is to circulate among the cutters and carver's assistants dipping from his *kendi*. We all bow to his brass ladle.

 WE WORK IN THE HOT SUN. From under his parasol over the east gate, Sastri (or his assistants) watch the come and go, alert to any slacking. We carve without rest, but for some brief moments toward noon when we are allowed to gulp our rice.

"Where are you off to?"

The assistant stops a cutter heading for the stair.

"To relieve myself in the meadow."

"And the new orders? Do they mean nothing to you? No one is to leave the gallery during the work hours. There is enough time to attend to your needs on your way up in the morning or down at night."

"What you say is so. But just now I am ill."

"It makes no difference. We can allow no one exceptions—by order of the *takshaka* himself."

Is SASTRI the one to issue these directives? Or are they issued from above? For example, this prohibition to leave the east terrace? I resolve to ask him once again.

"Sastri," I say, "before the many changes here, I came upon a way of working to take advantage of the light and cool. Could it be that I and my assistants may still be allowed to move freely around the terrace?"

"No one may have the run of any but the east gallery."

I try once more. "For example, this panel on the east side on which I work at present is sister to that panel of the west terrace showing Gopa's wedding. I have planned the designs from the beginning in such a manner that patterns repeat on all four sides, but with vastly different interpretations. In such a case, could I and my assistants be excused?"

"I myself see no objection to it, none whatever. But what is to prevent others from taking advantage of the same liberties? Besides which, it is not a practicable idea. There is only the one overseer's platform. How can we install one over each of the other gates with the few assistants I have at my command to staff them?"

 THINGS WERE DONE otherwise closer to home. There was a different kind of order. The raj gave his bond for our issue of rice. The brotherhood kept the lists, assigned the work, distributed the ration, buried the stoneworker when he died, sheltered the widow and orphan; even made a contribution each year for the upkeep of one temple or other.

I begin to have serious questions. For example, why the restriction to this one side? True, there is the matter of the deadline, an arbitrary one at best. And no doubt they observe the workers better from their vantage point. But perhaps it is altogether the wrong question I ask. Perhaps the question should be posed: why this side and not another?

What, for example, transpires now to the west, where the women have raised the new compound? Or to the south, where the defile of exhausted porters struggles between the riverbank and the growing pile of dressed stone which lies even now at the foot of the southern stair? Is it perhaps that the galleries have been closed off so that the cutters should not to see or hear? For what would happen if they continued to hear the lash, or could see the porters falter?

More and more I have need of the guidebook. The day comes when I am no longer certain of the carrying frame of a palanquin, or the gait of a horse. It is as if at last the monument had become my quarry; as if with each block grappled from the river, the temple had become the pit.

 I HEAR THE CUTTER just below my scaffold moaning in the morning heat. I lean over the edge the better to see. I recognize the fellow who asked to be relieved. Now he bends over a stone block retching. An assistant catches sight of him from the height of the observation platform. At once he hurries to his side.

"Get up," he hisses.

The man makes no move.

"Don't you hear? Get up."

The man moans faintly. A dribble of saliva issues from his mouth. The assistant prods him with the handle of his lash. His movement, however slight, is enough: the cutter falls to his side on the paving of the terrace. The assistant calls. His double comes running. They lift the unconscious cutter by the arms and legs to carry him away.

"Plague! It is the plague!" At the sound of this word, the cutters drop their tools. They congregate around the speaker, talking frenziedly. "I saw him yesterday. He was ill already then." But before they get much further, the assistant returns.

"Who gave you leave to talk? Does a little indisposi-
tion set you to chattering? Perhaps it is the whisper of
the lash you care to hear?" He paces up and down in
our midst. We return to work. The heat gives no quarter,
the sunlight no respite. It is not even noon and already
the air is thick with sweat.

THE ONSET OF the new monsoon is at hand. We hurry to complete the work assigned to us. The air hovers like a swarm of mosquitoes over a swampland. In a moment of rest, I stop to mop my brow. I let myself slide down from the scaffold. I back toward the parapet, the better to see, for the bamboo cuts off my immediate view. The panels in this section are nearly finished, for we keep to the schedule. I look beyond the shoulders of the assistants. Despite our cramped quarters, there is a certain consistency of motif, of treatment, a kind of integrity in which I pride myself. True, there are a few dead places. The horse, for instance, seems to have fallen stunned into a landscape of processions where before it swept flies off its rump while daydreaming in the fields. In this the *silpasastra* is of little help. I move toward the south corner, examining each panel carefully. I hear the assistant far behind me calling:

"Halt. The south is closed."

I am allowed to move no farther.

 UNDER THE DRIVING rain, we struggle to reassemble the scaffold on the western side, receiving the worst of this worst of downpours. Already in the first day's hubbub I misplace a mallet. I approach Sastri sheltering under his parasol. Despite the cover, he sits huddled under a thatch of his own making. Even the vast palm leaves cannot fully skirt his girth.

"Sastri," I say. "I must return to find my mallet where I left it. Will you escort me to the east gallery?"

He half rises from his perch, on the point of complying when he seems to have a change of heart. "Go yourself. You have no need of my company. You are quite safe. But be quick about it."

I move swiftly along the parapet in the pelting rain. I am not looking for it, but not to see it is impossible: far down below, circling the vast pile of rough-dressed stones left by the porters, the women struggle with the rollers. The overseers drive them in the rain. They work steadily, inching the stone from the south courtyard where the porters left it stored toward the eastern stair.

They are slipping in the mud, struggling under the weight, even now wedging the blocks toward the steep ramps that stretch beyond the galleries clear to the roof.

 I WORK AS MUCH as I can with a leaf of palm fastened over my head, without which seeing becomes impossible, for the rain runs down my brows into my eyes, dimming whatever the water itself leaves unobliterated as it shimmers over the surface of the stone.

My chisel is dull, the stone ill disposed. It, too, argues with the wet. Gopa greets me once again, refusing the wedding veil, unable to ward off the rain's assault, a long-suffering friend.

And Karto? Sometimes I still wonder about him. Has he made of his village a hiding place, or is he even now groaning under a burden heavier than stone in the high mountain above the clouds where it is said the quarry is concealed?

 THE WET ROCK steams under the relentless glare of sunlight. The monsoon is over at last. I am perched high in the scaffold when it opens: the earth begins a thunder not like any I have heard. Far in the distance beyond the limits of the jungle it comes rushing; in little more than a moment the roar is upon us. The stones seem to shift, to dance, as if they shrugged their shoulders, their backs to be free of it, like a wet dog snapping its skin, shaking it of wet. Those stones not already fixed by tenon joints bounce from the shoulders of the terraces: finials, balusters, all rain down upon us in the lowest gallery. It seems at once to last forever, and yet, perhaps in the turning of a head, it stops. Around me lie rocks, broken now, mere fragments. Everywhere people are running. Cutters lie screaming, some of them, or dead. There is blood on the paving stones. Sastri and his assistants are nowhere in sight. They seem to have fled.

All around, the bamboo platforms are shattered by falling rock, but the verticals, surprisingly, still stand. I scramble down; my knees, my hands must be shaking.

But it is the cutter pinned down beneath the pediment of rock screaming with pain that I bend over. How it comes to me, this strength, I cannot tell. A cube of rock as high as my loins, I roll it from him with a single sweep. He lies breathing now, groaning. His legs appear broken or crushed.

We free undamaged sections of the scaffold from the supports. Carefully we lift or roll the injured onto these. Throughout the day we carry them down the western stair, balancing them gingerly so they do not fall or slip. We move them across the courtyard onto the soft grass of the meadow.

We work without stopping, those of us who are unhurt, tending those who are wounded, removing the dead. We find the water carrier's *kendi* intact, still standing upright. We bring water to the parched throats of the wounded, the dying. The sun beats down with fierce indifference, making no allowance.

Toward night, we finish moving the wounded down into the meadow where we have spread matting for them to lie in the meager shelter of the sacred trees. At last I pull myself upright, stand pressing the palms of my hands against the small of my back. My body hums beyond weariness or exhaustion. For the first time this day, my eye takes in the mound, the wall. The terrace where I worked has begun to tilt dangerously outward. The stones of the basement wall supporting it have become rubble till there is hardly any courtyard left.

My mallet! I am running now, running toward the stair. It tilts dangerously. I take the flights two, three at one time. Alone now, the others gone—or dead—I stumble here along the buckled paving of the gallery. Dusk now, the twilight, it is barely light enough to see. But find my way, must find it (could do it already then blindfolded), for the stair leads me to the corridor. I round the sharp cut of the corner. There, in the darkest recess of the inner wall, under the ruined scaffold, I come upon my tools. But not by sight. It is too dark for that. By touch.

FOR MANY DAYS, I am unable to raise my chisel. I can barely circle the buckling terrace, examining the panels one by one. I dream of some distant harbor where a boat rides at anchor, waiting to return me to my birthright.

I am not anywhere near the galleries when Gunadharma comes. But Sintal, the assistant, tells me of it: "He moved about with his building assistant and the superintendents, taking stock of the damage during the entire day. Then he gave his orders: 'Bury the outer wall entirely. Cover the basement as it now stands with two measures of earth and rock. Thus shored, the foundations can support a higher balustrade.' "

For the supreme matter at hand—the shoring of the monument—must be planned, the workload apportioned. Direction is not long in coming. Of the entire population, three groups will be formed. All who carve or dress the stone are to become porters. Only master carvers such as myself are exempt. Quarrymen are to be set to work positioning the great stone blocks originally intended to pave the roof, against the foundations of the basement.

The panels on the western side, on which I have worked near onto seven seasons, will remain as I have planned them. Nearly half of them complete, they will be allowed to stand. For this gallery will now become the first: the carvings along the basement will be hidden from view by the shoring.

The north wall is the least damaged. It is on this side Gunadharma sets me back to work. By his personal intervention, I am allowed once more to construct a scaffold to replace the one destroyed by Sastri's order.

In the forest, the soil yields under the pressure of my feet. At last I find a bamboo grove where the growth is tall enough, although I must have circled it for some days already. I cut four staunch canes to serve as my verticals. I cut the reeds I will need to form the platform. I peel sufficient cane to weave the wattling. I balance the lot on my shoulder, tied with a length of fiber.

Close to my hut, I set to work. I collect enough fiber to lash the verticals together. I am occupied thus for several days, cutting bamboo, constructing my scaffold, the longest I was ever absent from the site.

 I SIT ALONE watching the fire. In the undergrowth, I hear a rustling. Alert, I sit upright. My eyes probe the darkness. Someone comes limping toward me in the firelight. Could it be Karto returned at last from his village in the valley? He is a shadow of what I remember. I barely recognize his face. It is worn, haggard. Deep furrows line his brow. Even by the fire's glow, I can see his skin has turned dark, leathery. I steady him and guide him to the rock close by the fire. I fill a bowl with gruel. I hand it to him. I am shocked to see his hands shake like an old man's. I watch him drink. I am afraid to question him. Has he come from his village? Or has he met the fate of the deserter?

"Have you escaped?" I whisper.

His laugh is bitter. "No need. They marched us here. Five days forced marching from the quarry. All the quarrymen, saving those who fell by the wayside." He shudders. "There is no compound here to hold us. We are to set a new foundation."

So that is it, I think. *Two measures of earth and rock.*

I settle him to rest on the floor of my hut. Through the night I wake to hear his groaning. So changed is he that even the *vardhakin* fails to know him when they meet. At night we share my fast-dwindling store of rice.

I watch as slowly he takes his strength. I ask him about his village in the valley. He shrugs. "No one was left but three old men. Nothing to eat. No rice. The fields were ruined. The work of my brothers, my father, all, all those before him—leveling the ground, building the dikes to hold the water, walling them with mud and dried grasses, draining the irrigation ditches after each harvest: nothing left. They could not feed one family. Not even one."

"And your mother?"

"Dead."

 I SURPRISE IT on the ledge, almost within handgrasp: a green lizard sunning itself. (It must have been spring for the light to have shifted.) The sun's slant will not betray my shadow. I hurl the mallet with all my might. The lizard tumbles convulsing off the ledge, the mallet rolling after it. It lies twitching in its death throes. A brown substance oozes from its throat. I seize the mallet, administer the final blow, my eyes averted in disgust.

It will make a welcome supper if I can conceal it in my *longyi*. For despite the widespread hunger now, the eating of animals is strictly forbidden.

 LIGHTING THE FIRE is no easy matter for there is no longer enough oil to leave the lamp burning through the daylight hours. I struggle with the tinder long into the darkness before the spark finally catches and moves slowly at first through the kindling I have gathered.

I clean the white flesh and impale it on the roasting stick. I stare numbly into the fire, waiting for it to sizzle. There is a stirring in the dry leaves at the edge of the clearing. Karto's stooping figure moves toward the fire. He is empty-handed.

"Karto! Where have you come from?" But my pleasure is mixed with knowing that he has come to share my dinner.

"Hunting. Like you." I see him fingering the hand snare, the kind they use hereabouts to trap small birds and snakes. "If we could only find their language to speak truth to lizards," he says, referring to the legend of the Manohara, "it would make things easier!"

"Like the hunter of the Manohara!"

I have not forgotten the jest, or his reply:

"So you remember the story?"

"Of the Manohara? Of course!"

"Of what happened to the carver."

"The carver? No."

"And Gunadharma has never talked of it, of course."

I am puzzled.

"It was the carver of the lion and the jackal."

I search my memory. It seems so long ago.

"We went to see the wayside shrines. You stopped, stood for a long time before the panel. . . . It was the first day of your coming."

"The lion and the jackal!" Now it comes to me.

"Everywhere they searched. He who would carve the memorial to Sudhana must be without peer. In vain. They found no one equal to it. Then at Mendut they discovered him, scarcely more than a boy still then."

I wait for Karto to continue. Even wrapped in the fire's glow, I begin to shiver. I am uncertain why.

"You remember the day? We reached the courtyard, were to pass within. At the bottom of the stair, there was a solitary beggar who, even then, stretched out his hands . . ."

". . . begging for alms . . ." I gasp my unbelief. "But he was blind!"

"No. Not blind. . . . Blinded!" I feel my hackles stand on end.

"But why?" I gasp.

"Why? Because such perfection must not ever be

repeated. The Sailendra made sure of it: 'Spare his life (for here we have no cruelty). Only blind him, send him into darkness.' "

A long silence settles between us. At last, "Karto," I whisper, "I would give a year of my life for each one of them, twenty years of working in this hell to have brought forth those twenty panels."

"But your seeing?" He eyes me for a long time. Is it anger I see in the sharpness of his look?

 I<small>T</small> I<small>S</small> S<small>AID</small> work heals. And perhaps it was so for me. For on the morning, when I return, my scaffold strapped to my back, something in me has changed. Is it that I am forgetful of Karto's story? Is it that I convince myself the warning does not apply to me? That as a foreigner I am safe? I am no longer sure.

This I know. Before resuming work, I pause this morning at the eastern stair. I prop my scaffold against the lintel of the gate. In the section which stretches toward the southeast corner, the stone blocks, already secured by tenon joints, have withstood the shaking of the earth. The capstones and finials still stand. I lean against the parapet, allowing my eye to run over the panels. Of the upper row, I know every mallet stroke that went to make them. Below, my eye plays over the legend of the Manohara. Behind me, the sun rising bathes the stone in rosy light. The figures seem to breathe as though, for this magic instant, they are released of their stone fetters, able to move at will, to speak. Maidens bend at the water's edge, filling their brass vessels in the murmuring stream. Overhead the raucous cries of macaws startle the jungle air. Sudhana bathes at the stream's edge. And I watch—in the brambles, a jackal envying the lion's splendor.

The sun lifts higher, my shadow obscures the panel; the light is gone, the moment vanishes. On the north terrace, no rosy light will ever bathe the Blessed One who wades the sacred river. I wonder, even if it did, would it be as enchanting by half as this ablution of Sudhana's?

I work as doggedly, perhaps with even greater energy, now that Sastri's deadline no longer drives me. One by one, my young assistants find their way back to my side, all but the one whose legs are crushed. And for some days now, none of the superintendents are in evidence. Despite my hunger, I have not worked with as light heart before—or since.

 Is THEIR ABSENCE the result, as some would say later, of the growing disagreement between Gunadharma and the overseers, particularly the *vardhakin*? Or because Sastri finds himself more and more caught in the middle by their arguments? Or is it simply that the Sailendra themselves have come to find the endless years of building tiresome? I cannot tell, but as a lull remains only as a memory, an eye of respite at the storm's heart, so this time of working beyond the watchful eyes of the superintendents. It is not to last.

There is no more rice. I remember Karto's words of long ago: without it, there is neither food nor life. Nothing of beauty is possible anymore. At first the overseers issue millet to supplement the difference. In the compounds, the population swells. There must be some eight thousand, all needing to be fed and sheltered.

Aside from the carving, all other work ceases, whether of laying the roof pavement, boasting capstones and finials in the upper balustrades, carving the latticework for the rooftop shrines, or forming the images

1 7 7

of the Blessed One designed to fill the niches and the hidden stupas of the roof. For many days (although we have no way of knowing why till later) Gunadharma and his building assistants meet with the overseers, with representatives of the guard and of the court. It is for this reason they are all but absent.

Sastri and the *vardhakin* have little time for me. All day, I carve to the sound of rock cascading against the foundations where, since the departure of the quarry-men, the women have been left to pour it by the basket-load.

 IT HAS BEEN said the roof was made, not of rock, but gruel. But there comes a time when, like rice, the millet, too, runs out.

From the height of my scaffold, I catch sight of a curious procession. A growing line of bullock carts invades the meadow. At first I have difficulty making out what it is they carry. Only as they come within earshot of the gallery, when I can hear the jangle of the harness bells, do I recognize the freight: over one hundred cauldrons so vast they can have come only from the palace kitchens.

The dedication is brief. A Sailendra princess presides—she who is the donor of the cauldrons—over the first feeding line. The ceremonies are unmarked by fireworks or even kite flying, for the workers are hungry. And indeed, the porters working the remote reaches of the river are unaware they take place at all.

 ALL MIGHT HAVE BEEN well had it not been for Sastri's order that the workers continue marking for their ration, although there remained no rice or millet with which to feed them. To that end, he had constructed an overseer's booth in full view of the Sailendra guards' pavilion. And among the workers, was it not common knowledge that the guard received its ration from the palace stores?

One evening, I hear a curious sound—a flapping as of whole flocks of water fowl. Who can imagine a sound more innocent? And I, unsuspecting, turning to the parapet to see. Far below me in the meadow, vast numbers of workers mill about, tearing, wrenching, ripping down the overseer's booth. The *vardhakin* comes running. They seize him and with a great shout, they hurl him thrashing and howling into the steaming cauldron. The rage! I hear them shouting still. And the guards outnumbered, swinging their swords in their vain attempts to quell the frenzy. The mob stampeding, overturning cauldrons. People trampled, steamed to death.

And the guards are powerless to stop it. The mob fans out, heading for the compounds, setting them on fire.

In the morning, I can see horsemen gallop through the smoking ruins, clubbing workers to death. Some, less fortunate, are chained and taken prisoner. But not many. From the north terrace I watch them being marched across the meadow under guard.

Peace of some kind is restored at last.

THE *VARDHAKIN'S* cremation ceremony becomes an occasion of rededication. Gunadharma sits high on the overseer's platform, presiding in his monk's robes. Beside him sits the king—the only time many who have worked here year after year ever see him— and that from afar. For none are permitted to enter the shrine. All are assembled in the low-lying field—where the Sailendra guard can watch for any sign of restlessness.

Shortly thereafter, when I go to receive my own reduced ration, I discover Sastri's hut has been removed from its site beside the worker's compound to safety within Mendut's temple courtyard.

LATELY I HAVE come to wonder had the Sailendra some part in drawing up the battle lines. For all knew the guards received their ration from the palace stores. There were some two hundred guards to control some eight thousand. Curious how those in power conceive of schemes the least countryfolk would ridicule as senseless!

On the face of it, the results seem devastating. But at the same time they bring about the new order. They have the effect of cutting the compound population in half although some, like Karto, are reassigned to the roofing crew. They put a new regime of palace guards in power whose first act is to close the compounds once again: there is to be no more foraging, no uncontrolled come and go. And in each gallery, a watch is mounted by the guard.

Sastri is supplanted as overseer. His function is reduced to that of quartermaster. And I continue to have to walk as far as Mendut once every seven days to obtain from him my ration.

You may ask where I stood amidst the tumult and the shouting. But for myself, other than a certain inconvenience, the events leading to the coming of the new overseers affect me only slightly.

In the west terrace, calm returns. I have the supplies I need, and the assistants I require. I am free to forage at will. I still make my own fire, cook my own rice. For my hut lies in that part of the jungle to the east. I pass neither compound nor overseers' huts on my way to and fro. Only Gunadharma's hut stands in some proximity to my own.

Of such upheaval, I think: it is none of my affair. Let them settle their own scores one way or another. For I have been promised my share of gold at the successful completion. I have worked here nearly fifteen seasons. I care only to see the terrace carving through to its conclusion.

 ONE MONSOON succeeds another. Work on the west side nears completion. Once I have readied the panels for the painters, Gunadharma assigns me once again to the eastern terrace. Sometimes, as I work, I can hear the foremen chanting, pacing the porters by the river bank as they heave blocks onto the rollers. For the final effort is underway: the roof will be complete.

If anything, in all this time I have come to prefer the guard watch to the overseers. True, they are soldiers, thick-necked ruffians whose training is all mayhem. True, they brook no interference. If a worker makes trouble, they may seize him by the neck in the breathless vise of an armlock, may shake him until he no longer remembers what disturbs him. Or failing that, they may simply hurl him off the parapet to let him bruise or break his bones below.

But they know nothing of incising, of carving, of backgrounds, or of subjects, and unlike the *vardhakin*, they know it. With my work, they never interfere.

 Surely the dawns cannot have been as chill, the stone as gray, as shrouded in fog, the stairs as endless, or the terraces as blanketed in mist as I remember. The day's first sound, the pad of my footfalls, the dull thud of the carrying cloth, the clink of chisels unwrapped, the fruitwood mallet. Only these hard things have stayed to remind me of that other place—for even my garments have become strange, unlike any I wore closer to home. Only the chisels remain now, yes, and the memory: cold dawn, chill light, the stone guarding its secret. And the chisels.

 THE TIME COMES when my ration no longer lasts me through the week. I return to my darkened hut at dusk. I crawl inside and stretch out on the mat. I close my eyes. I try to sleep the hunger off. My nights are filled with dreams of feasting.

It is in such a time I lie only half awake. A silhouette fills my darkened door.

"Master."

Who can it be?

"Master," he beckons.

I come outside into the open. It is Karto. In the time I have not seen him, his hair has turned white.

"Master," he says. "I have brought someone."

He has never called me thus before. I rub my eyes awkwardly. I think to myself: you have eaten the last of the rice, drunk the last of the palm wine. There is nothing left, will be nothing for some time. And curiously, although my stomach has not forgotten hunger, I am not troubled by it. My teeth have become quite dark. The betel stains no longer rub off. I have changed, of that I am sure. My hair is graying at the temples. But surely I have not changed so much as he. I am grateful for the darkness. I am tired, too tired to imagine anything, whether of eating, or of wanting anything. I have long ceased my dreaming of the harbor, of the ship that waits to take me home. For now home comes to me only in dreams. My sons? Would they know me? Or my wife who left me? Or that other one, she of my heart? Gone, all gone now. Lost. Dead, perhaps.

I throw some dry twigs on the embers. Karto says nothing. Does he, too, dream? Does he remember the rice once lying fat and swollen on the beating stones? Or his mother singing knee-deep in the water?

"Master," he says, "I have brought someone with me."

I stare at him blankly. For there is no one there. Karto, himself, is little more than a ghost.

"Permit me to call her."

"Who is it?"

"She is my wife." In the many seasons I have known him, I never knew he had a wife. He lets out a call into the darkness of the jungle, a call like a night predator's, like an owl's perhaps. The night stays quiet, undisturbed. Again he calls. But even before he turns back toward the smoldering fire, I catch sight of her. The woman is standing quietly at my side. How long has she stood there like that, I wonder?

"I will sell her to you," he says.

I am dumfounded. "But she is your wife!"

"I will sell her to you for one measure of rice."

1 8 8

I turn to the woman. She is thin, so thin she appears tall, yet she comes perhaps to my shoulder. She carries a bundle in the fold of her garment. She stands watching impassively. She does not look directly either at me or toward Karto.

"Only one measure."

"I have nothing left with which to buy her."

Karto casts a quick look at my empty hands. Then: "But we have had nothing *longer* than you." Still now I remember his words. For some time he stands staring impassively into the fire. Then: "Wanting her is enough. I will leave her to you."

Before I can stop him, he lunges, stumbles toward the underbrush, without looking back. There is no time to protest.

"Run," I say to her. "Run. It is not too late. You can still catch him."

She stands quietly, without moving.

"If you run, you may catch up with him. Even now! Go!"

But she makes no move. Instead, she lets go the bundle she holds tightly fastened in her garment. Brass cookpots and bowls scatter to the ground as she falls. In the darkness, I pull at her hand, grasp her by the arm, struggling to get her upright. She is dead weight. Some sudden anger wells up from a place I no longer recognize.

"Get up! Get up!" I scream. "You can't lie down here, I have nothing! Nothing is left in the storage jar! Don't you understand me? Get up! You can't stay here.

Go. Go at once. And take your vessels with you!" I try
to gather them up but they fall from my grasp and clatter
to the ground. "Get up! Get up!" I shake her senselessly.

For all my outburst, she continues to lie still. I stoop
to look at her more closely. Her eyes remain shut. She
lies as if sleeping in the swirling disarray of her garments, amidst the deluge of cookpots and serving bowls
which lie empty, their brass glinting dull gold in the
firelight.

What can I do? In the clay vessel there is still water.
I fetch it now, touch a few drops to her temples, to her
lips. I wait, squatting at her side, fanning her with the
palm-leaf fan.

After some time, her eyelids flicker open. She gazes
at my face, lit as it is by firelight. She lies without
expression. Only because of the fire's glow am I able to
catch the lone tear that strays across the hollow between
cheek and brow. I am abashed at my outburst, relieved
that she must not have been witness to it. I cannot think
of what to say. At last I say, "My name is Gopal."

She smiles faintly. "They call me Prenguseng-
Poan."

Then, as now, I cannot say her name. But she is
content. I have other means of summoning her when I
require.

"You cannot stay here in the damp. I will spread a
mat for you on my sleeping platform. Tonight. But tomorrow we will go in search of Karto to bring you back."

On the morrow, as I mount the stair toward the
fourth gallery, through the stone arch I have a furtive

glimpse of the first circular terrace, the flags already laid, and already dotting its periphery, the lotus mouldings waiting for the hoist to burden them.

But when I inquire for Karto of the building foreman, I find he has vanished. He is a member of the roofing crew no longer.

 I VISIT SASTRI once night has fallen.

"What brings you here ahead of schedule?"

"There is something of which I must speak to you. I have taken to wife a native woman."

He waits, one eyebrow raised expecting to hear what I will say.

"We require rice in larger measure now there are two mouths to feed."

He smiles. "Yes. But have you received approval of the bond?"

So it is with such "approval" they control the come and go of their own people, conserve the dwindling supply of rice.

"No such restrictions apply to foreigners," I say, sure of myself.

"Yes. But the woman is not foreign. You yourself call her native. And besides, you being foreign, you and she are not bound to our custom—nor we to you! Where does she come from?"

I see his subtlety, his deviousness too late. But there

is no stopping now. I have walked long into the night to come here.

"She is with child," I say.

I UNTIE THE handful of rice from the fold of my *longyi* where I have kept it for the long walk back. I let the few grains rain down on the hollow stone she has set before the fire. It is late. She sits on her heels beside the fire. Her eyes shine, wide with pleasure at seeing the rice. Over the fire, a pot has been set to boiling.

"We will save it for a time when it is needed," she says. "There is enough for now without the rice."

She lowers a ladle into the steaming liquid. She pulls it up and offers it. "Smell," she says. My eyes fill with steam, but the smell is sweet. "What is it?"

"You will see. I will prepare to serve it to you."

I gather my tools together, place the bundle on the sleeping platform. I take down the clay jar from its sling in the rafters. I notice it is full, not half empty as it was when I last used it. I pour a few drops to clean my fingertips.

She sweeps the last grains of rice into the small brass bowl before preparing to serve me supper.

"Where does it come from?" she asks.

I crouch at the fireside. "I will tell you." She places the bowl before me. I smell its contents once again as I tip it to my mouth. Despite the steam, I sip. It is like nothing I know. A taste of meat, gamy, some sweet taste with it. She sits watching me, her eyes shining. She will eat later when I am done. But clearly she is proud of her triumph. She must have tasted it from time to time as she awaited my return.

I sip cautiously so as not to burn my tongue. When the mixture cools enough, I reach into the bowl. I find a piece of meat flaking off the small bones of some animal. A bird, I think, or frog.

"Where did you catch it?"

"In the forest. Many times it passed, close, so close, before it sprung the snare!" She is clearly pleased. But then I recognize the paw, the five long toes, still intact, the pad flaking off, the claws: it is a jungle rat, and these soft things must be roots she dug. How long, I wonder, has she eaten such things. Lizards are delicacies—compared to this.

"And the rice? Where did you get it?"

"From the quartermaster," I say. "From Sastri."

"Is he your friend?"

"Sastri? Sastri is no one's friend if I judge correctly. No one who rations rice . . ."

"Is it a favor, then?"

"To me? He gives no favors. Not Sastri. I had to tell him a story."

"What did you tell him?"

"That I had taken a native woman to keep my house."

She eyes me with alarm. "What else did you tell him?"

"That you were with child."

I hear her sharp intake of breath. Her face knots up. "Was it wrong to say?"

But she is silent. She runs a hand over her rounding belly. How can I have missed noticing?

"How long is it?" I ask her.

"Five, maybe—almost six months now." She is quiet, troubled. So Karto knew. This is why he left her with me.

"I didn't know," I say. "An impulse took me. . . ."

"To tell him?"

I nod. I see her troubled look. "What harm is there?"

"It is nothing," she says. She seems to shake off some dark vision. "I only fear what they may do."

 I RETURN JUST BEFORE SUNDOWN to find her not alone. In the hut there are midwives. There is no sound from her, only the dull thud of their hands and fists beating against the ripeness of her belly. They have been at their task since early morning.

"Stop," I order.

They stare at me blankly. Without letup they continue to beat her. When one wearies, another takes over.

"Who sent you?" I demand to know.

"The overseer from the compound."

"You cannot beat her. It is my child she carries."

"What is that to us?"

They go on as though they could not hear me, as though I were not there. There is nothing I can do to stop them. I see her lying helpless on the mat, her eyes tightly closed. With each blow, her face tightens. But she gives no cry. The midwife pauses only long enough to wipe her own brow. She works barebreasted, the better to withstand the heat. When she tires another takes her place. The beating continues with barely a noticeable break in rhythm. Her face winces, the eyes remain shut. The dull thud of fist on flesh continues. I can watch no longer.

I huddle bent over beside the darkened firepit, cold, and without light. I have forgotten eating, forgotten hunger. The wind taunts me with the rattle of palm fronds. I can hear the pound of fist on flesh even at this distance. I shut my eyes. I dream of Durga singing, at work pounding the rice.

What air is this heavy? and behind the
oleander, who is it bends over the beating
stone, pounding the rice? The pole argues
with the mortar: who is it threads the thin
song on the lips of the wind? thwack, thwack,
husking the grain?

I start awake. I hear the blunt thud in the darkness, the rhythmic laboring. I am reminded. Now it is she they husk, emptying her of seed. There is no other sound. Through the wattling I can see the midwife bent to her task, swinging against the flickering lamplight.

The path is visible only here and there in the moonlight. I am running, not mindful of any direction, not thinking, plunging nowhere headlong. Of a sudden, the shrine looms before me, black, silent, forbidding in the moonlight. I mount the north stair, not stopping, not considering the presence—or absence—of the guard. I pass under the dragon canopy, cross the first gallery, still running, scale the upper galleries until at last I burst

198

through the last stone archway. I stand panting, alone on the windswept summit. But no. Not alone. For there, each one of them mounted on their lotus mouldings, waiting for the stone latticework to veil their nakedness, they sit, a dark circle lit by moonlight, sitting in silent contemplation, the Blessed One as his own disciple, in a vast mirror company, image after stone image, identical, not moving, and clasped in each stone hand the wheel of law, spinning, still, still spinning for eternity.

I am no nearer them than if I stood once again in my own country, yet from where I stand I can reach out to touch the one whose back is nearest me. It is as if a hand propelled me forward until I am lying in their midst, prostrate on the cold flags of the highest circle. *Know, O my brothers,* I whisper, *Know, I my brothers, this life is pain. Pain in the coming in, pain in the going out.* But I can go no further. Something foreign holds me back as if their great circle sat in silent judgment. For all the while, I know I am calling up one more ancient, less known than these. *Siva,* I whisper, *Siva, let it be over. Let it end now.*

I remember nothing of returning. Near the fringe of the clearing a cry comes to me. A long, seemingly endless wail trembles on the night-chilled air. Not bird, or beast, or even the screech of owl can rival it. It is done. A sigh goes up, words are spoken, laughter wells up, is choked back. A sob. I hear them stirring. Their footsteps set the mat to rustling. In the iron light, I watch the first of them emerge, and then another. I enter the hut. She lies on the straw mat, her face all but obscured. She appears to sink into the floorboards, to become one with the mat. They have covered her with her *longyi*. At her feet, the last of them fumbles with a straw bundle. Through the fibers, a faint ooze of red appears, then fades, as once more the straw absorbs it.

 SHE LIES, barely breathing, her narrow chest more hollow than a girl's. Sometimes her eyelids flicker. I bring her water. She is too weak to drink.

A day passes. I make gruel. I offer her some. She shakes her head. Her brow glistens with sweat. I touch her cheek, her neck. She burns like fire. It cannot last much longer like this. I wonder where I will bury her.

I lie awake, eyes closed. I cannot hear her breathing. I think: my trouble with her is at an end. My eyes are sealed shut. Can it be I do not want to see her body lying there, no more solid than a child's? Or is it perhaps some stirring of regret? I start up. The place where she has lain is empty.

"You," I shout. "You!" Where could she have gone?

Outside, where she squats, relieving herself in the clearing, I hear a thin sound, more like a whisper: "Here. I am here."

 SHE HAS BEEN WITH ME since then. I can still remember my feeling of relief. Relief she was still living? No. Still there? Not either. Not then. Relief only that I had not seen a ghost. From this time perhaps came our . . . but no. Thinking now about how it was with us, we have only briefly . . . We have been as husband and wife only briefly, and that much later. For in truth, at the beginning, I was not drawn to her in that way—perhaps because Karto thrust her upon me when I could least accept her presence.

She was a long time healing. She would sit by the fire saying nothing. I boiled what rice we had. Every day it seemed to me that there was less in the jar when I returned.

Of the midwives, nothing more was heard. But the mystery stayed.

"Is it to all who are with child they do this? Is there so little left they must take food from the mouths of those unborn?"

"No. It was not because of the hunger. It was because I ran away. Because I went to join my husband."

"You were in the women's compound?"

"From the beginning. From the time they first came to our village. When they took Karto, they took me also. Took all but those who were too old to work."

So it was I found I had been mistaken. For the overseers did not imagine to put an end to birth but to make of her an example because she had escaped to find her husband.

"Why not return to your village, now?"

"Don't you want me here? Don't you want me to stay with you? I can find food. In the open, I can forage. I can cook for you."

"And Karto?"

"He is gone. He left," she says sadly. "I don't know where."

"Perhaps in your village."

"No one goes there anymore."

"How can you be sure of it?"

"Because they had to eat the seed. When there was nothing else. There can be no more planting there again."

She bends over the fire, stirring the gruel. From time to time, I hear a hissing where her tears fall in the flames.

 ON THE ROOF they have begun to set the latticework. In the first gallery, all is complete but the northeast section, those panels which lie to the right of the east gate.

She is in the way of women, again. What draws me, I cannot tell. Her scent, perhaps. I move toward her slowly, would embrace her in the darkness, but my hand running under her pillow touches something grainy, something wrapped in cloth. She awakes gasping, for I have her forearm in a vise.

"You have taken it! It was you who took the rice! All the while, it was you!"

"Please, please do not hurt me," she pleads.

I lash out in a fury such as never before took me. I remember nothing like it ever—before or since. I seize her by the forearms, I hurl her backward, screaming in terror, down the deep stairs of the *pendopo*.

She lies in the not yet light, whimpering. I let her cry. I let her lie there, affecting not to hear or notice. I lie upon my mat. I cannot sleep. My fury knows no bounds. I smash my fists against the wattling.

What seized me I no longer know. I fumble beneath her pillow till I have the wrapping cloth by the knot. I run to the doorway. I hurl the grain out into the night. It whips through the air in milky loops pelting her like rain.

She flies at me, wrestling me in her grip. "What! What are you doing with the seed?"

In the great force of her fury, she knocks me off balance. I fall to my knees. I am dumfounded that she who is so small, so silent, could become this white fury, could hold all this in a body little bigger than a child's.

"I was saving it for seed! All this while I served you, while I found food, while I cared for you, each night. I took one grain of rice! Was this not my due? Count them! See if you can find them in the grass to count them!"

 I RECOGNIZE THE restlessness that is the sign: the monsoon is about to break. I lie on the mat in the small *pendopo* where I sleep, listening to the change in the cry of birds making ready, the shift in the voice of the wind riffling the grasses.

"Will you come with me before the rain this time while I gather grass for drying?"

She lies beside me on the mat. Her question sets me to thinking. There has been little work of late, fewer people dying.

"We can take a cart," she says. "You will be comfortable. By night you can sit close by the fire where you can warm yourself."

I consider. I cannot remember being absent from the work mat since we came here.

"And if I am needed?"

"There is enough stored. There is no need for concern. I will ask the neighbor to watch while we are gone."

Our LIVING here is not easy. Far from it —not since the coming to power of the Sanjaya. For they are worshipers of Śiva, god of my country, not of the new religion. They have left us the ruined capital, preferring to settle in the east.

One could argue that a master carver, once a *silpin* at the height of his powers, with a reputation throughout the southern provinces, has no call to end thus, to find himself here in this boarded-up backwater, a valley of such depletion it is now farmed—what is left of it—in shifts. But in adversity, it seems somewhere there is benefit. In some curious way, I find this carving of funerary ornaments lively enough. For one thing, it feeds us, her and myself. For another, little more is left by the departing Sailendra—besides ruin—but death. For come what may, death remains a certainty. That is amusing in itself when you consider: for although it overtakes us all, it also visits the Sailendra.

But there is still another reason, that in its way outweighs the others: for now these trivial furnishings demand more skill than did the vastly complex frieze that still stands two days distant, offering its marvels to the invading tendrils of the jungle.

SOMETIMES CURIOUS passers-by stop beside my work shed and whisper among
themselves, "How does he do it?" I am
not angered, for now their question,
which in former times could vex me to distraction, is
quite welcome. I must confess it: I am satisfied, much
more pleased at my resourcefulness than ever I was at
my skill.

I let them watch for a time. Then I say: "You want
to know how it is done?" I rise from the mat, move to
where a fresh stone stands, dressed and ready. I measure
with three fingers up from the ground and drive a mark-
ing exactly at the spot, then rotate the stone until I have
marked it thus on all four corners.

"Now I am ready to carve the base. When the foot
is done, I will measure in the same way upward for each
new molding until the finial is complete."

"But how to keep it true?"

"With the stick." And I show them the vertical
marker she has fashioned for me with its bristling set of
minute calibrations against which I take the measure of
the stone.

 I FEEL THE AIR on my cheek. I have been in the shade of the work shed too long. The cart jolts along the path. I smell the dust.

"You have been awake of late—as if you knew no rest."

How can I tell her? It is not even clear to me. Sometimes, I believe it is only the shadow workings of my mind gone dark. There is nothing to tell, no sign to go by.

"I must roam the galleries again, calling the panels to mind."

"Perhaps we can return some day?"

"Return?"

"Perhaps some day. I can lead the way . . ."

I ponder this thought of hers. *No*, I think. *Never. Never there again.*

"Perhaps," I shrug. "Sometime."

"Are you afraid?"

Her question brings me up short, as if the cart had jolted, nearly thrown me to the ground.

"Afraid? No," I say, "it is not that."

But I feel her silence more keenly than her question.

 PERHAPS AFTER ALL, I was undeceived. Perhaps I understood Karto's warning all too well. His story of the eyeless carver was clearly meant for me. Lying sheltered in the *pendopo,* neighboring what had once been Gunadharma's hut, she and I, listening to the ceaseless drumming of the rain, it must have been I knew. Yet there was no escaping. *(Manohara, O Manohara, if you be the daughter of King Druma, stand still!)* Where would I go? What would I do? There was nowhere. Not the rice fields surely, ruined, their dikes bruised, caved in of neglect. Not among those left who even now must lie in their huts moaning of hunger—or of the plague that waited till it was impossible that anything be left living to take the rest.

I must have known they would come for me from the time the earth shook, was it?, when I slowed the carving, spent whole days looking, taking stock of what was done and what was left to do before once more taking up the chisel. Perhaps already then I began my efforts to delay the end, the time when the agents of the Sailendra would come at last, would say, "Gopal, you have finished. You are now ready. We are ready for each other," would say, "Now there is nothing left for it: you must come with us."

**THE ROOF IS** all but finished, the latticework shrines, the last great stupa, all complete but for the image of the last, the secret Buddha, whose hand is always raised in blessing, yet never complete. But this morning, strain as I may, I cannot see it. The fog hovers low, revealing nothing.

I begin at the east gate (as I had that first morning in the company of Gunadharma, when we first mounted the stair, saw the barefoot women straining under their basketloads. *Where are they now?* Only the stair remembers, wet and dismal in the downpour.) Let me gaze once more on this splendor—is it possible? But how? In these long seasons—twenty monsoons—how is it possible that this world came from my chisel, this world that waited for someone to quicken it one day: the great processions, the offerings, the giving of alms, the dreams scented with illusory flowers, the soft flesh, the drone of the master's voice, the fiery wheels striking sparks from the stone? And here by the south gate, Queen Maya being comforted in childbed—her deathbed—by a sister who was perhaps a stranger?

The rain digs channels along the hollows of my cheek. It is too wet for tears, or if I shed them, I would not know. I round the corner. The west gallery is flooded for the drains no longer draw. They must be filled with the dust and dead matter of these many seasons. I come upon Gopa once more, Siddhartha's bride. Perhaps Maya, too, should have refused the veil, the house, the bed, would herself have run wild in the never-ending fields of childhood, never to learn tears.

It is all here, all of myself, in these apparently public ceremonies—performances, Gunadharma called them— every secret moment of my being, the particles which, taken together, must make a life—what is called living.

I turn the corner. The Bodhisattva bathes eternally in the sacred river, the small fry frolic in the stream. *See it, trap it, see if you can catch it in the stone!* Do they know? Is this the thing perhaps that men call life, this bowl of light set to rocking by the hand of someone— a child, perhaps, a stranger? Is this what they mean? For I can see only the bowl, only the light rocking, forever rocking against the rim, now seeking, now re-pelling the sunlight.

I round the northeast corner. *Know, O my brothers . . . this life is pain. . . .*

Then I see them, all three, their *longyis* soaked and clinging, lounging there, in apparent unconcern despite the downpour. They are waiting for me by the eastern gate, where the hand of the Holy One, still unfinished, is raised in blessing.

 SOMETIMES NOW, especially when I am at rest, when my hands drop idle in my lap, still now, I think about the hands of the Blessed One, unfinished, raised in the gesture of teaching, the night not over, the sermon not yet begun.

For in reality, although I worked more than twenty monsoons to close the round, the end approaching took on the dread of an abyss looming before me. Perhaps I sought to forestall the coming of the dawn—before the Holy One began to preach. All was complete when the rain began, all but the hands.

Rain slowed the friability of the stone, made it sullen. Soon water dulled my hammer blows. Having come full circle, the east side sheltered me once more, as it had at the beginning. Still I worked. I stopped only when the tier above began to shower water in my eyes.

Still now, I think about the hands, unfinished. Is the gesture clear? Do you, seeing it, know the story is not yet complete?

THE TIME CAME when Gunadharma was no more. At first it was believed he had retired to the abbot's house, some two day's journey from the site. Perhaps there was need of him no longer. Perhaps some foreign project claimed him, for, with the coming to power of the Sanjaya, there was no longer need of an architect of his belief.

Still now, there is a story I have heard tell about him here. It is said that when the brigands came and tore open the roof shrines, laying the lattice stupas waste, they tried to penetrate the topmost shrine. They found the stone door sealed fast. Try as they might, they could find no way for their crowbars to wedge it open.

No one knows quite how, but I have heard it said that Gunadharma was brought there captive secretly at night, was made to tell its secret. And when the shrine was open at last, they sealed him shut, alive within it.

I myself know nothing of this. But this I know with certainty: the image of the Holy One, his hand raised in blessing, has been found. It lies no longer in the secret chamber, sealed for all eternity, but on the riverbank near the site where someone who could no longer carry its great weight, abandoned it.

 I CAN SEE THE rosy tongues of flame lick the shadows on the vault above me. And they, intent on their struggle. The oil lamps light their faces fleetingly. With the strips of my *longyi*, they lash my hands together behind me. They kick me onto my back. I can see them more clearly now. Curious at first I fail to recognize him: but of course! It is Shanggal. With the absence of the veil, despite the years, I know him well. A wasting disease has attacked his face. The nose is hollow.

"The feet. Tie the feet," he urges. There is a smell of fish fermenting on his breath.

Rigid as I am, I can see someone working at my feet, feel the hands busy with my ankles, the lashing again and again.

"Bind him fast."

I smell the fire, acrid, of iron, rusty, heated to red heat in the brazier.

"Quickly!"

Someone runs across the stone floor, spilling little tongues of flame. Someone is rushing at me. I see what it is they are about.

"No!" My scream still circles back from the darkness to meet me, even now. Over and over. "No."

The darkness catches fire. Inside, outside, the red bursts into green. It goes shrieking in my skull. Pain, not knife, or stone, or fire, none of these. Pain has become me. And darkness.

 THE CART shudders to a stop.

"What are you thinking?" she wants to know.

I shrug. "The sound of metal, the sound of metal on stone. 'Clink, clink.' Still now I hear it whenever I stop."

"Only when you stop?"

"Only for a moment. Like a shadow of light when the eyes are closed after looking at the sun: all that was green turns red. And all that was red turns green."

She whips the bullock. The cart jerks forward once again.

"I could have sworn you were looking at an echo."

 I OPEN MY LIDS. Pressed to the mat, I lie still as one shipwrecked. Fog, oblivion cloud my waking. It is morning. I hear the dawn wind riffle the bamboo. I feel an itch, an insect perhaps. I raise my hand. But no. My fingers come upon the wet. Always it astounds me that the face, deprived of eyes, still weeps. But for the first time, I might never have discovered it. I sleep like a stone now with no memory of dreaming, yet here the tear lies puddled, trapped in the curve of nose, of cheek, trace of a separate life, closed to my waking. I wipe my cheek, turn over on my back. I can hear her singing in the pavilion as she hangs the grasses from the cross-beams.

What could it be I wonder? Something, a child's voice, my own perhaps, cries out somewhere within me, reminding me of exile. From where does it come? From what recess, long buried?

One word: "Gopal!"

But who? It is dark. No one comes, no face. Can it be no one is left? Have I run out at last? But no. Some

warmth, some arms, as of a body pressed to mine. Someone at last, wiping the blood from where it cakes about
my eyes. What were once my eyes—hollow now. I hear
it now, the sobbing. Mine? Mine, too? What? What
now? Some . . . some life still in these bones, this flesh?
Some stirring? Some sound at last?

I WONDER IF I could see her now, would I find her beautiful? I think not. She has let me feel out her face until I know it well enough to carve it in the stone, or summon it at will whenever I desire. But this heavy stolidness, shaped by coming age, by the practice of the everyday, the bending, the sweeping, the face all but hidden, wrapped in the patience of the daily rhythm, the even broom strokes, pounding the rice flour, arms quivering to the thud of pestle against the stone, raising a hand, perhaps, to brush off the sweat, or to lift the straying tendril from the eyes; pouring oil into the vats, or the squeal of winch that tells me the play of arms as she draws water, raising the jug to shower my head, my neck, washing, drying, flapping the clothes free to air out in the sun, spreading them on a bush to dry. Shelling, husking, squatting over the cooking fire, fanning the flame, the arm occasionally raised, the elbow lifted to ward off the straying lock of hair, is this beauty? Is it her I really see? Or do I imagine it?

 OUTSIDE it has begun to rain. I hear her sandals in the dust. For a long time she stands there beside me. I sit on the mat, the tools idle, sunk in my lap. I imagine her standing there listening to the rain.

The runoff sounds a measure in the hollow of the cistern. Over and over. Is it some melody? Some tune I cannot recognize? I begin to hum.

Then it comes to me:

MAIN STUPA

5. TERRACE

2. TERRACE

1. TERRACE

PLATEAU

4. GALLERY

3. GALLERY

2. GALLERY

1. GALLERY

HIDDEN BASE

MAIN STAIRCASE (SOUTH SIDE)

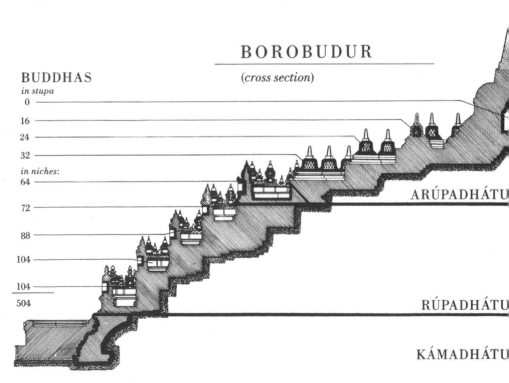

BOROBUDUR

(cross section)

BUDDHAS
in stupa

0

16

24

32

in niches:

64

72

88

104

104

504

ARÚPADHÁTU

RÚPADHÁTU

KÁMADHÁTU